COUNTRY LEGACY

HER STUBBORN COWBOY

Patricia Johns

P9-API-970

HARLEQUIN

HARLEQUIN®

Recycling programs
for this product may
not exist in your area.

ISBN-13: 978-1-335-52333-4

Her Stubborn Cowboy
First published in 2016. This edition published in 2022.
Copyright © 2016 by Patty Froese Ntihemuka

For questions and comments about the quality of this book, please contact us at CustomerService@Harlequin.com.

Harlequin Enterprises ULC
22 Adelaide St. West, 41st Floor
Toronto, Ontario M5H 4E3, Canada
www.Harlequin.com

Printed in U.S.A.

Patricia Johns is a *Publishers Weekly* bestselling author who writes from Alberta, Canada. She has her Hon. BA in English literature and currently writes for Harlequin's Love Inspired and Heartwarming lines. She also writes Amish romance for Kensington Books. You can find her at patriciajohnsromance.com.

To my husband,
who inspires the romantic in me.

Chapter 1

Chet Granger wanted her land, and Mackenzie Vaughn knew it. He'd offered to buy it from her grandmother multiple times over the years, and now that her grandmother had passed away, leaving the ranch to Mackenzie, she was waiting for the inevitable offer.

And she would refuse. That was a given. The last person in this county she intended to sell this land to was Chet Granger. They had a bit of a history together, and if anyone was going to benefit from this land, it wouldn't be him. Business wasn't supposed to be personal, but this time it was.

As a small white goat passed her, Mackenzie patted its rump and wiped the back of her hand over her moist forehead. The sun hung low in the sky, casting long shadows through pools of warm sunlight. The peeling red barn loomed behind, its shadow stretching out like a sleepy cat. Since arriving two hours earlier, she'd already managed to get what was left of her grandmother's herd back into the barn. Then she'd noticed the goat waddling off toward the fence, wide belly swinging back and forth with each step.

"Come on now," she urged. "Let's go, goat."

It had to have a name; she just didn't know it. The other three goats were already inside the barn, but this one paid no mind to peer pressure.

This ranch had been a godsend when she was an angry teen caught in the middle of her parents' acrid divorce. While her parents battled over who got what, she'd come back to her grandmother's ranch—the one place she could count on not to change. It was here that she'd fallen in love for the first time, with Andy Granger. Chet was Andy's older brother and had always been the more serious of the two. In fact, she'd had a bit of a crush on him at first, before Andy made his move and she realized that Chet hadn't been interested in the least. He'd been concerned with the future of his family's ranch more than with having much fun...so much so that he'd convinced Andy that Mack wasn't worth his time. At least, that was Andy's story. In spite of it all, a small part of her envied the Granger boys. When push came to shove, they chose each other, and the Granger family stood strong. Still, they stood strong against her, and that was one slight she wouldn't forget.

"Come on," Mackenzie coaxed, patting the goat's rump again. "I have some nice fresh hay waiting for you."

The goat didn't seem the least bit interested in her offering, and it turned away again, trotting heavily along the fence line. Farther down the fence, a man sauntered up and leaned against the rail, gray eyes fixed on her in mild amusement. Mackenzie startled. He was tall, slim but well muscled. He rested his forearms over the top rail, big hands loosely holding a pair of work gloves. A cowboy hat sat on his head, pushed back so that the sun hit his face, illuminating the sandpaper of his stubble. He raised the gloves in a hello. He'd always been good-looking, but he'd lost his lean boyishness and hardened into a man since she'd last seen him. Chet Granger. The years had been good to him.

"Long time," he called.

It certainly had been a long time, and in the few hours she'd been back, she'd been doing her best to avoid him. She'd known that wasn't going to work for long, considering their ranches were side by side, their respective barns and houses no more than an acre apart. There had been a time when people liked the idea of being within shouting distance of a neighbor. This would have been a whole lot easier if they didn't share such a difficult history.

The goat trotted up to Chet and poked a nose through the fence.

"Hey there, Butter Cream." The rancher eased between the rails of the fence and came over to her side, hopping twice to get his boot through. His shirt was rolled up to reveal strong forearms, tanned skin with a vein bulging as he scratched the goat's ears. The animal tipped her head back and forth, lashes fluttering in enjoyment. Chet looked up at Mackenzie, those disconcertingly light eyes pinned on her. "Trying to get her back inside?"

He didn't wait for the answer but strode off in the direction of her barn without a backward look, and the goat followed him with the quiet loyalty of a dog.

"Butter Cream," she muttered to herself. That would be good to remember for the next time she had to plead with this particular critter.

Mackenzie had been in town all of a day, and she already knew that she was in over her head. Why she'd thought she'd be able to run a ranch on her own, she had no idea. When her grandmother had died, leaving her the ranch, she'd thought this was the answer to that sense of empty boredom inside her—and maybe it was—but she wasn't entirely sure it was worth it, especially not if Chet was part of the package.

"So how come you didn't stop by when you arrived?" Chet glanced over his shoulder at her as he pulled open the rolling door.

"I had things to do," she said, annoyed at his casual comfort with her property. And it *was* hers now—all four hundred acres of it.

He laughed softly. "You have no idea how to run this place."

He was right about that, but she'd never been one to back away from a challenge, and this one had been dumped in her lap with the subtlety of a truckload of bricks.

The goat nuzzled Chet's leg once more and he bent to scratch her head again. "By the way,

Butter Cream is due to kid in a week or two. So pretty soon, you'll have baby goats and a pretty steady supply of goat milk. She's a good producer."

Mackenzie studied the creature, attempting to hide her surprise.

"As in more than one?" she asked.

"Definitely more than one."

"I don't need goat milk," she said, before she could think better of it.

"Then sell it." Chet gave the goat's rump a solid pat, and she waddled through the door toward her stall without a bleat of protest. He made it seem so easy, and she suspected that she'd never have that kind of luck with Butter Cream.

"Do you want her?" she asked. "She seems to like you."

"No, thanks." He pulled shut the goat's stall door and shot her a grin. "Do you have any idea how much trouble baby goats are? They're like herding cats. They're your problem."

Great. She pulled a hand through her long blond hair. "You're right, by the way."

"About the goats, or about you not knowing what you're doing?" His grin became teasing.

Mackenzie eyed him coolly. "Both, I'm sure." She sucked in a breath. "The lawyer said that you'd been helping my grandmother out with running the place. He said I should talk to you if I had any questions."

"Good advice." Chet crossed his arms over his chest.

"So?" she said. "What's the first step?"

"Your grandmother—rest her soul—sold off most of her cattle at auction a couple of years ago. That was her version of retirement. No ranch hands, no employees and just a handful of cows she could care for on her own. But you can't keep this place going on fifteen head. You'll need a good herd and some ranch hands who know what they're doing, and you'll have to be careful with that. If they think you don't know squat about running this place, they'll take advantage."

Ranch hands were the least of her worries right now. Was he going to try to scare her off running this place on her own? No one had been more shocked than she'd been when she inherited this place. If anyone was going to get it, it should have been her father, and that fact had been rubbing at her conscience ever since the lawyer had called. She was the least qualified member of the family to inherit the biggest responsibility, and this was already affecting her relationship with her dad.

She scuffed a boot in the dirt, her mind sifting through Chet's words. She had no idea how she'd get this ranch rolling again, and right now she felt most thoroughly beaten. "In the meantime, what do I do?"

"Chores in the morning, chores at night. In between that, you fix everything that keeps breaking." He glanced through the barn. "Looks like you got the cows in all right."

The cows had taken care of themselves, trotting inside without a word from her when she opened the back barn door.

"I understand you've been paid for your time out of the estate," Mackenzie said.

He nodded, silent.

"And you know how to run this place better than I do," she went on. "I'm not sure what you'd want to be paid, but—"

"I don't want to be paid." He let the words hang in the air, then turned and walked back toward the fence. His boots clunked against the dry ground, and he lifted his hat and resettled it on his head without once looking back. She knew what he was after. He wanted to buy this place and send her packing. Still, he'd had a point about being taken advantage of by employees, something she hadn't even thought of. She needed help.

"Chet!" she called.

He paused and finally looked back at her. "Yeah?"

She'd make him say it. She'd make him offer to buy the place, turn him down flat and get that out of the way. "So what do you want, then?"

"To be asked." There wasn't a hint of humor in his expression.

She blinked. That wasn't what she'd expected. "Fine. I'm asking."

"The whole thing." He crossed his arms, meeting her gaze evenly.

Mackenzie muttered an oath under her breath and closed the distance between them. Was his plan to prove to her how little she knew about managing a ranch? If it was, then she'd just have to prove him wrong—learn everything she could from this frustrating man in spite of his reticence.

"Chet Granger," she said with a resigned sigh, "would you be so kind as to help me with the running of this place until I can figure out what to do with it?"

"What do you mean, what you're going to do with it?" he asked.

There it was. She'd piqued his interest. Maybe her father would want to buy her out, although besides being deeply hurt that his own mother had cut him out of the will, he hadn't shown a lot of interest in this place.

"Obviously, I can run it or sell it. I haven't decided what I'm going to do yet."

"But you want to run it?" he clarified.

She nodded. "That was the plan."

She had a lot of regrets that needed plowing over. She wanted a fresh start, and a ranch didn't land in a girl's lap every day. This seemed like the kind of thing she should take advantage of. She was hoping that her father could forgive this eventually—but if she were honest with herself, the philanderer had a little karma due.

"All right." He fixed her with a direct stare. "But I put my ranch first. I help you out after I'm done with my own land."

"Fair enough." She held out her hand and he took it in his strong, rough grasp.

"I'll come by after my chores are done in the morning." He released her fingers, tipped his hat and then bent down to ease his body between the fence rails once more. Once he was on his side of the property, he added, "And I'm not doing the work for you. I'm teaching you how to do it yourself. But I'll help you out for a bit while you build up the stamina. It's harder than it looks."

"Do you really think I'm searching for a man to take care of little ole me?" she asked wryly.

"Just being clear."

"I'm not looking to get free labor out of you, Chet," she said. "And I'll pay you for your time. I won't have it any other way."

If she'd had anyone else to ask, she would have, but Mackenzie didn't know anyone around here but the Grangers. When Andy broke up with her, he'd told her enough to make it clear that Chet had been at the core of it. She'd always sensed that Chet had never thought she was anything more than a city slicker, and he'd never approved of her wasting Andy's time when he should have been thinking about more serious things like animal husbandry and crops.

Andy hadn't cared about the ranch the way Chet had, and that had always chafed between the brothers, but she'd never thought that Chet would go so far as to break them up. That was a low blow—lower than she'd thought Chet was capable of. But then, her father had proven himself even lower, so perhaps she shouldn't have been surprised.

Chet gave her a nod. "Good to see you again, Mack," he said. "You look good."

Then he turned toward his own property and

walked across the field with that slow, rolling gait of his. She heaved a sigh. She needed to figure out how to run this ranch on her own or sell it to anyone but a Granger. And being beholden to Chet wasn't even an option.

Chet's side kitchen window overlooked the field that separated his property from Mackenzie's, and he stopped in front of the sink, casting his gaze over there in spite of himself. He pulled his eyes away and slammed a kitchen cupboard just to hear the satisfying bang.

Mackenzie Vaughn was back.

He hadn't been sure if she would actually come and take possession of the ranch or sell it without setting foot on it again. Of course, he'd hoped for another chance to see her, but he'd never understood Mack very well. She'd been pretty and tomboyish with long blond hair and even longer legs. She hadn't changed much in the past decade, apparently.

He'd thought the years had washed away the memory of her, especially when Chet took over the running of his family's ranch. He'd been busy, focused on upgrading old machinery, so life had moved on...

Until he saw her again this afternoon, trying to sweet-talk a goat into cooperating, and

it was as if those past ten years had just evaporated. Suddenly he was nineteen years old
again, staring at the girl who made his stomach
flip, knowing he couldn't do anything about
it. She had been Andy's girlfriend, and there
were lines he'd never cross. Except she wasn't
Andy's girlfriend anymore.

The rumble of an engine came up the drive,
and Chet ambled through the kitchen toward
the front window. A brand-new blue pickup
crunched to a stop on the gravel, and when
the door opened, he blinked in surprise to see
his brother. He hadn't spoken to Andy in the
year or more since their father's death, and the
sight of his younger brother made his throat
tighten. After the funeral, they'd had a massive fight over the inheritance and things had
been said—the kind of things that couldn't be
taken back. So what was Andy doing on his
doorstep? Was this a friendly visit, or was he
here to pick up where they'd left off?

Chet pulled open the front door and gave
his brother a cautious nod. Andy, shorter than
Chet by several inches, slammed shut the truck
door. He was tall and well built—the family
resemblance between the two men was unmistakable, except that Andy's hair was auburn

in a testament to their redheaded mother. He shuffled his boots in the gravel.

"Hi," Andy said.

"What's going on?" Chet asked. "I thought you weren't talking to me."

"Ida kicked me out." Andy slapped his hat against his leg. "I was hoping I could stay here with you for a few days until I get things sorted."

"What do you mean, kicked you out? The wedding is in two months, I thought." In fact, Chet wasn't even sure if he was invited. Ida had sent him the invitation, and he suspected she was trying to be diplomatic. That didn't mean Andy wanted Chet anywhere near the event.

"We broke up." Andy gave a weak shrug.

"What did you do?" Chet demanded.

"Can I stay here?" Andy asked, ignoring the question.

"Well, you're here," Chet said gruffly, which was as close to a yes as Andy was going to get. Andy grabbed a suitcase from the truck's flatbed and Chet stepped back and let his brother through the door. "So what happened?"

"I asked if we could postpone the wedding a bit. It's in two months, coming up so fast, and—" Andy's face looked older now, more lined and haggard. "You were smart to stay single."

Chet wasn't so much smart as unlucky in love. He'd dated a few women over the years, but in a place the size of Hope, he'd known most folk all his life. A few new people moved in every few years, but most of them were older or with young families. You didn't get a lot of available women putting up their shingles in a place like this.

Andy strolled toward the kitchen, and Chet followed. This was their family house—they'd both grown up in it—and treating it like a shared home was a hard habit to break. Chet had inherited the house, the barns and one hundred and seventy-five acres. His brother had inherited the other two hundred and twenty-five acres—mostly pasture—and their shares combined to make the Grangers' four-hundred-acre total. Their father's intention had been for the brothers to run the ranch together, except that Andy had never been interested.

"So it's over, I guess," Andy went on, opening the fridge and peering inside. "You don't have much, do you?"

Over. His brother had been dating Ida for four years, and it was simply done? This was the first woman Andy had brought home whom the whole family really liked. He turned his attention to the fridge.

"What do you want?" Chet asked. "How about sausage and eggs?"

Andy shrugged his assent and headed to the battered old table, where he sank into a chair. Chet set to work in the kitchen. He grabbed the eggs and sausages from the fridge and moved around getting what he needed. Andy scrubbed a hand through his reddish hair, leaving it standing upright.

"So just like that?" Chet asked. "You sure this isn't a fight? Cold feet?"

"She's not the right woman."

"You thought she was when you proposed," Chet said. That had been before their father died and while everyone was still talking to each other. Andy had used their mother's engagement ring. Made sense—Andy had always been close to Mom. Chet had been out on the land with their father, and Andy had seen a lot more of their mother before she passed away, something Chet had always felt a little envious of. Had he known their time would be limited…

"A lot changed in the last year," Andy muttered.

A lot *had* changed, but truth be told, Chet had been slightly jealous of his brother's good fortune. He'd fallen in love and was getting married. What better way to get over the death of a parent than by starting your own family?

"Speaking of that year," Chet said. "I haven't heard a peep from you." He hauled an iron skillet onto a burner and turned it on.

"Well...peep."

Chet rolled his eyes. He'd have to take what he could get. He'd missed his brother, gone over their fight over and over in his head, looking for some fresh insight into why they fought and how to fix it and always coming up empty.

"Dad should never have split the land up like that. It wasn't fair," Andy said. "Not that you'd notice."

"You got more land than I did," Chet retorted. "You got all the pasture. It's worth a good chunk of change, so don't go acting the victim like Dad didn't remember you."

The pasture was in Andy's name, but Chet had been using it just as their father had used that land before him. Chet had always looked at the ranch as theirs—his and Andy's—but it was no secret that Chet was the one to run the place and do the actual work. Andy was more of a silent partner, and Chet liked that setup just fine.

"I meant to talk to you about that," Andy said, squinting. "I'm going to sell it."

"What?!" Chet slammed a spatula on the counter and stared at his brother in disbelief. "You can't do that!"

"Totally can," Andy replied. "It's in my name, and like you said, it's worth a small fortune to the right people."

"Yeah, but it's our pasture," Chet said. "Where are we supposed to graze two hundred and fifty cows if you sell it out from under us?"

Andy shrugged. "Maybe this isn't a great time to talk about this."

"No, this is a perfect time," Chet said. "This ranch needs land. You know that. I can't run the place without it."

Andy pulled out his phone and punched away with two thumbs for a few seconds, then passed the phone over. "This is the development company that is interested in buying the whole lot—yours included—for more money than we'd ever get otherwise. We'd be rich."

Rich. That was what Andy wanted—cash? Rich was when you had land under your feet that you owned free and clear. Rich was when you could stand outside at dawn and watch the sun rise over fields you owned as far as the eye could see. Rich wasn't about a fistful of cash; it was about something deeper, more meaningful. It was about roots and history, being connected to the living expanse of something bigger than yourself.

"I'm not selling," Chet said. "This is ours. This means something. The Grangers have been on this land for generations."

"Then maybe it's time to try something else," Andy said. "Think about it. There are more opportunities out there than you even know about, and with that kind of money—"

"I don't need to think about it," Chet snapped. "I'm not selling."

"Okay, then." But there was something in Andy's tone that Chet didn't trust, the same vibe he'd given off when he was planning to do something he knew he'd get in trouble for when they were kids. More often than not, Chet waded in to try to fix it and ended up in trouble, too. But not this time. They were adults now, and the consequences went far deeper than a month of grounding.

"Are you selling no matter what?" Chet asked cautiously.

Andy nodded. "Yeah, I am. I love this town, too. I know you think I'm some unfeeling jerk. You're not the only one with childhood memories in Hope. Our parents are buried here, so don't go getting all high and mighty on me about family and land and all that garbage that you love to lecture me about. I don't want to stop here. I only get to live once, and I don't want to regret turning down that kind of cash. It could really open doors."

Chet had no idea how life could get better than what he already had, but this had always been their problem. Chet loved this land, and Andy just wanted to get a few bucks to escape to the city. Andy wanted fun and Chet wanted stability. They'd never been able to see eye to eye, not even as teens.

"Then sell it to me," Chet said.

"Are you willing to match their offer?" Andy leaned over and pressed another button, pulling up an email. The number was far larger than Chet could possibly get credit for. He felt his stomach drop.

"You know I can't match that," he said. "But I'll give you what it's worth, fair and square."

"*This* is what it's worth now," Andy said, slipping his phone into his pocket.

"What are they going to do with all that land?" Chet asked.

"They're going to make a resort, apparently," Andy said. "There are all sorts of rich people who want to pay good money for a ranch experience, but they want to be comfortable at the same time."

The very thought turned Chet's stomach. But his brother hadn't sold the land yet. Andy tended to talk big, and while he wouldn't put it past his brother, he still had hope. Maybe Andy's mind could be changed yet.

"Don't jump into it," Chet said. "I'll buy you out if you let me. Just…" He sighed and didn't finish the sentence. His brother knew exactly what this would do to him and ironically—or obliviously—still wanted a place to stay.

"I'll think about it," Andy agreed. "But you do some thinking, too. This could be good for us—really good. You're always so tunnel-visioned, but if you gave this a chance—"

"I told you. I'm not selling." Chet couldn't help the sharpness to his tone.

They fell into silence for a few beats. It had always been like this when Andy was around. He managed to take a calm, serene day and turn it into an argument.

"So when are you going to apologize to Ida and go home?" Chet asked, changing the subject.

"I'm not." Andy sighed. "It's definitely over. She gave me back the ring, and I'm hiring movers."

"I'm sorry," Chet said gruffly. He felt a wave of sadness. He'd miss Ida. She'd been a great addition to the family.

Andy nodded somberly. "Hey, you remember that girl Mackenzie—the one I was head over heels for?"

"Yeah."

"I should have married her while I had the chance," Andy said, his voice low.

Those words sparked anger deep inside Chet. Andy hadn't appreciated what he had when he had it. Mack had been sweet and gorgeous, smart and funny. She'd been the whole package, and Andy had started up with another girl behind Mack's back. When Chet told Andy that he knew what was going on and that it wasn't fair to either girl, Andy had agreed to choose between them. Chet had been sure that he'd land on the side of Mackenzie, but he hadn't. He'd dumped Mack with little ceremony and carried on with some girl he'd met at the county fair. And now he was looking back thinking that he should have married Mackenzie? Mackenzie was lucky to have gotten away relatively unscathed!

"You're an idiot," Chet said. "You cheated on her."

"I *was* an idiot," Andy said. "I was also seventeen, and I've grown up since then. If I had a chance with Mack again, I wouldn't squander it."

What terrible timing. He didn't have the stomach right now to tell Andy that Mack was back, mostly because he was pretty sure he'd clock his brother if he even mentioned going on over there to talk to her. But he couldn't keep Mackenzie a secret for long. Still, some things could wait for another day. He had his brother back, and irritating though Andy was, Chet had been hoping for a reconciliation every single day for the past year. Family mattered. So did engagements, come to that.

"Ida's worth some effort," Chet said. "Four years. That's a lot to throw away. Go grovel."

"She said she'll really miss you guys, too," Andy said, turning away from the window. "Hey, but this is what lasts, isn't it? We're brothers. Women come and go, but we Granger boys stand together, am I right?"

"Yeah, until some development company comes along," Chet said, bitterness edging his voice.

"You could make a fortune, too," Andy said, sitting down as Chet put a plate of sausage and eggs in front of him. "Try something new, Chet. Take a chance. I want to do this together."

He glanced out the window toward the house next door, the roof of which was just visible from where he stood. Mack was back and so was Andy, and they were already resuming the old roles they used to play. Andy was breaking hearts, Chet was holding together the ranch, and Mack was—

Mack was what, exactly? Mack, still as gorgeous as she'd once been, with that ornery streak and the defiant way of facing him down that made his mind go into dangerous territory. And there was still a very solid line between him and Mackenzie. Only this time it wasn't about being too principled to make a move or about keeping the Granger family united. It was now about keeping his ranch. Because if he ticked off his brother this time, Andy had the trump card—he had a juicy offer to buy his land, and he didn't need Chet for that.

Chapter 2

The next morning, Chet got up earlier than ordinary and slipped out of the house to start his chores. He was eager to get outside again after an evening with his brother—at least, that was what he told himself. It would be ridiculous to get up an hour early to rush through his work so he could get to Mack's place as soon as possible… Ridiculous, plain and simple.

That morning, he'd snuck around the kitchen like a ninja, not wanting to wake up his brother with the sound of cooking. Andy could get his own toast whenever he roused himself. The night before, they'd stayed up late, Chet listening as Andy made the case for selling their family's land and starting fresh with some new venture. Andy had obviously put a lot of thought into this scheme, and his business degree hadn't been wasted. There were statistics about profit and loss, land equity and… Chet couldn't even remember all of it. All he knew was that he wasn't selling, no matter how good the deal might be. This land wasn't about cash; it was about roots, and Chet wasn't about to be budged on that.

The chilly morning air mingled with the last dregs of his coffee. He drank it black and strong, the same way his dad used to take it. And when he pulled on his boots and dropped his hat on his head, he felt the same peace that flooded through him every morning. It was something to do with the smell of the barns and the sound of horses nickering before they could even see him. Or maybe it was the way the sun eased over the horizon as he lifted bales of hay into the back of the work truck— a twelve-year-old Chevy that was mottled with rust but still going strong. It was hard to pin down exactly what settled into his soul so perfectly, but this was the life for him.

He and Andy used to do chores together as kids, but there had been more than a few mornings when Andy was let off the hook—normally for a feigned stomachache—and Chet went out with his dad alone. He'd cherished that time. His father had been a quiet man who'd kept his own counsel, but when he and Chet would walk out to the barn together, his father would talk. Chet was the first to know about his mother's cancer because his father had told him one morning in the field.

It wasn't all heavy talk, though. His father would tell him stories about the Granger men who had come before him—working this very land under his feet. There was the grandfather who'd drunk himself into an early grave and a great-uncle who'd bought the most westerly section for ten dollars and a jar of preserves. One ancestor had been a ranch hand on this land and ended up marrying his boss's daughter—Matilda Granger, if he recalled properly—and running the place for his father-in-law until the old man died. The ranch was then left to a Granger cousin instead. This land had been fraught with conflict and grit, and hearing the stories had made Chet feel as though he belonged with the rough group of men who had worked the land before him. As a kid listening to the family lore, he'd never imagined that he and his brother would be part of that Granger conflict, but remembering those stories now, he sensed the irony. Apparently, this land came with an ability to cause strife.

Chet's chores went faster than usual, and after giving a few instructions to his ranch hands, Chet drove over to Mackenzie's place. He didn't know exactly what he was expecting today, but he was definitely looking forward to seeing her. This was different from before. She was a grown woman now, not a naive girl, and he found himself wanting to get to know her all over again. She was the same old Mack, and yet she was so much more now. Was it crazy of him to entertain these thoughts?

I'll be her friend. I'll help her out. That's it.

That was what he kept telling himself, at least.

Mackenzie was waiting for him on the wooden steps. She cradled a mug of coffee between her hands, and her hair was pulled back into a ponytail so that her face was fully exposed. She looked more vulnerable that way, her blue eyes lighting on his truck as he pulled up. She put down her mug and waved.

"Morning!" she called as he turned off the engine and hopped out. "You're earlier than I thought."

"I got an early start," he admitted. "I was

pretty eager to get out of there. My brother showed up last night."

"Andy's here?" She frowned, and he wondered what that meant to her. She'd been pretty smitten with his younger brother back in the day. "What's he doing with himself now, anyway?"

"He lives out in Billings," Chet said. "Manages a car dealership."

"And why did he come here?" she inquired, squinting up at him from her perch on the steps. She shaded her eyes against the morning sun.

"He, uh—" Chet cleared his throat. "He had a bit of a falling-out with his fiancée. He's out here to cool off and I'm hoping they'll patch it up."

"He's engaged." It wasn't a question, and she looked away when she said it. "I hadn't realized that."

Well, he had been. Close enough. Sometimes it was better not to nail down any definitions and give a couple the chance to fix things if they wanted to. He was still hoping his brother would change his mind.

"Helen never told you?" Mack's grandmother had been very much alive when Andy had gotten engaged, and she'd had her own opinions about the relationship. Helen had declared Ida sweet but unsuitable, which Chet had never agreed with. Ida was good for Andy.

"You know Granny. She kept me on the need-to-know. I guess she didn't think I needed to know that."

Helen hadn't wanted him to tell Mackenzie about Andy's cheating, either. Helen's son was Mack's father, and he had been cheating on his wife for years—hence the divorce. Helen loved family fiercely, but not fiercely enough to cover her disapproval when it came to infidelity. She'd said that Mackenzie had enough to contend with in her parents' divorce and she didn't need to develop a complex over cheating men, to boot.

"Let sleeping dogs lie," Helen had said.

"Except Andy isn't a dog," Chet had said pragmatically. Andy couldn't just be chained up or taught to heel.

"Isn't he?" Helen had fixed him with a demanding stare, and that was that. They'd agreed to never tell Mack about Andy's cheating, and it looked as if Helen had taken that a step further and never mentioned him again, period. Helen was ferociously protective of her grandchildren.

"Yeah, Andy met Ida a few years ago and they've been dating for a long time. He finally asked her to marry him about a year—maybe a year and a half—ago. She's this artsy yoga instructor, and she's laid-back enough to deal with Andy. He can't flap her. They're good together."

"I imagine they would be." She nodded briskly and pushed herself to her feet. "Let's get to work."

Technically, his duty was done. He'd given her the pertinent information about his brother, and she could take it from there. But he wished that Andy didn't have to be a part of this. When Chet learned that Mack was inheriting her grandmother's ranch, all those old feelings for her had come back. And he wanted a chance to see her again without his brother in the mix. Maybe it would be a simple hello and that would be it, but Andy was supposed to have faded into the background of engaged bliss. He was supposed to be out of the picture.

As they made their way toward the barn together, Mackenzie stayed half a step ahead of him, and he wondered what had brought her out here, besides the inheritance. The last he'd seen of her was when she left the ranch after Andy dumped her. She'd given him this unreadable look, then gotten into the truck, and Helen had driven her to the bus depot. That was it. As far as Chet knew, her last memories of Hope, Montana, were of heartbreak—a heartbreak that Chet couldn't even explain to her, because it would only hurt her worse. So why on earth would she come back?

The small barn closer to the house was normally where horses and smaller livestock were housed, but when Helen sold off her herd, she'd moved the remaining cows—her bottle-fed babies—into the smaller barn, leaving the big high-tech barn empty.

Mackenzie pulled the heavy door open, and it took all of her body weight to do it. She obviously wasn't going to let him take the lead, and he liked that. The more seriously she took this, the better the chances of her succeeding on her own, and staying...

Was he hoping for that? He told himself that he didn't want to be wasting his valuable time teaching someone who wasn't going to stick around, but it went deeper than that. He wanted her to stick around. The minute he saw her yesterday, something had sparked to life inside him that had lain dormant for a long time.

Chet followed Mack inside the barn and looked around, impressed. Mackenzie had mucked the barn out that morning—it was obvious by the smell of new hay. The cows knew their way to the pasture, and they were already gone, as were the goats, who would never allow themselves to be left indoors in summer weather. The stalls were clean—a few details missed here and there, but an admirable job for a first-timer. This was several hours' worth of work, and he looked over at Mack with new respect.

"Let me see your hands," he said.

Mackenzie blinked at him twice, then held them up—gloves on. He laughed softly and plucked the gloves off. She held her arms straight, palms down, as if he'd asked to inspect her nails. He took her slender wrists and turned them over so that he could get a look at her palms. They were red with blisters—a sign of hard work. Her soft skin wasn't used to this, and even through the gloves, she'd gotten some punishment.

"That'll hurt," he said, his voice low. She bent her head, looking down at her skin, and her hair shone warmly in the dim light. He could smell the fragrance of her shampoo, in spite of the barn aroma around them. He pulled his mind back from those details. He needed to keep this strictly friendly if he knew what was good for him at the moment.

Mackenzie closed her fingers over her palms. "I'll toughen up."

She pulled her hands back, and Chet cleared his throat.

"Looks like you got a good start on the day," he said.

"I was up early, too." She cast him a wry smile. "I remember Granny used to say that the animals needed to be clean and dry. I saw to that. Also, they looked antsy, so I let them out."

"Did you find the feed bins?" he asked.

She shook her head.

"That's fine while they can graze. But they'll need food overnight. You'll have to know how to mix it—especially for the herd, when you get one again. Basically, Helen was using a mix of chopped hay, corn silage, soybean meal and some fruit rinds that she'd been getting from a grocery chain for next to nothing. It's just recycling for them. It takes a bit more to separate it out, so they charge a minimal amount..."

Mackenzie followed him as he walked down the aisles, pointing out how the place would work differently with a larger herd. He loved this stuff, and he found himself rambling about feed control, disease testing and signs of a sick animal. Cows had been his life for as long as he could remember. He'd grown up next to them, and while he worked on instinct a lot of the time, ranching was a science and it was absolutely teachable. It didn't hurt that his student was so attentive and pretty…the soft scent of her wafting through the other smells and taking him by surprise when she stepped past him.

"I'll have to give you a walk-through of the big barn," he said, and when he turned, he nearly collided with her, and they were suddenly barely an inch apart. She sucked in a breath and looked up at him, blue eyes widened in surprise. Her lips parted as if she were about to say something, and he found his eyes moving down toward her mouth as if closing that distance would be the most natural thing in the world.

"Sorry." He cleared his throat and stepped back. The thing was, this wasn't his "turn" with Mack. Mack was a woman, not a hand towel, and the fact that he'd felt things for her back when she'd been dating Andy didn't mean anything. People felt things all the time, and they didn't act on them.

"So what brought you out here?" he asked, mostly to change the subject.

"You know why. I inherited it," she said simply.

"It's more than that, though," he said. "I mean, you only visited for a couple of summers, right? Most people would have sold it and taken the money."

She moved a coiled hose aside with her boot. "The timing just all came together in the right way. I hated my job. I've been working at an insurance company that paid pretty well, but the job was just soul sucking. I missed air and rain and land and—" She blushed. "You always thought I was a city slicker, huh?"

"Yeah, maybe." He grinned.

"And I am. I admit it. But even people in the city miss a connection with something real…"

He was real, and what he'd felt for her had been real, too, but he'd never let her see that. Family was real, too, as were irritating younger brothers who moved in on every available woman.

"And these city slickers go to resorts to find it?" he asked drily, his mind back on the sales proposition his brother had shown him. What a load. Connecting with the land wasn't quite so sterile as some people hoped.

"Maybe," she said with a shrug. "But when I got the news that Granny had died and left the entire ranch to me, I just had to try it, you know. I don't think this is a chance I'll get more than once in my life, and I think Granny left it to me for a reason."

"Helen was like that," he agreed. The old woman hadn't done anything without praying on it, as she put it. "But when you left, things weren't…exactly on great terms."

"Andy, you mean," she concluded.

"Yeah, Andy. We Grangers don't hold pleasant memories for you, I'm sure."

He couldn't quite decipher her expression. "What makes you think that my most meaningful memories were with Andy?"

She meant her grandmother, of course, and Chet nodded. "Good point."

"I mean, he was my first real love, and that's special, but I wasn't going to walk away from a chance like this because I happened to date a boy the next ranch over." She shrugged. "That would be stupid, wouldn't it?"

After they checked on the animals in the field, Chet provided the promised walk-through for the big barn. Chet was helpful and informative. That in itself was suspicious. Why would Chet, the man who'd never thought her good enough for a Granger, put his valuable time into her ranch unless he had an ulterior motive? He'd offered to buy this property repeatedly over the years, and she had to wonder if his interest in keeping up her land was more selfish than he was letting on.

Chet opened the front door and gestured her

outside first. Her arm brushed against his taut stomach as she passed by him and back into the sunlight, the warmth of his body just a little too comforting for her liking. But then, she'd always been attracted to Chet. He'd been the silent, brooding sort, but as it turned out, connecting with a man like that was difficult, especially when his more outgoing younger brother was pursuing her like crazy. If Chet had felt anything for her at all, he'd hidden it well, and she'd let her feelings for him go when she'd started dating Andy. As it turned out, she'd done the right thing—he'd never thought she was good enough, anyway. She'd only have made a fool of herself, and no woman in her right mind courted rejection.

Granny had made this all seem a whole lot easier, and she'd hired and fired her workers without apology. She'd had some simple rules on this ranch—no booze, no sleeping around and no cursing within her hearing. She knew that ranch hands had a rare talent when it came to profanity. Far be it from her to tell them what to do on their own time, but if she was even around a corner, she expected them to clean up their language pronto. There was something about the sight of that slender woman with gray hair and gum boots that made the men stand up straighter and doff their hats. Every single ranch hand Mackenzie had ever seen around this place called her Granny "ma'am," and while she wasn't sure how exactly, she had the distinct impression the old lady had earned it.

Granny, I wish you were here to give me some advice...

Granny wasn't, but Chet was. He'd have to do.

"Come on," Chet said as he led the way to her truck.

"Where to now?" Mackenzie asked.

"The house. We'll take care of those blisters."

He got into the driver's seat, and she felt a pang of annoyance. He was already acting as though he owned the place, but her hands were quite sore. A couple of blisters had popped. She'd let this one go. For now. But she wouldn't back down, and she wouldn't let Chet push her into any corners. This was her land now, and if she was forced to sell, she'd sell to anyone but him. On principle.

If there was one thing that her father's infidelity had taught her, it was that men could lie. Before her father's affairs came out, she'd trusted in a man's good intentions, but not anymore. If her father could look her and her mother in the eye and tell them that he was so sorry, but he had to work late... It had been a painful lesson, but a valuable one. Men lied. Men looked out for their own interests, and a woman should never rely on a man to care about hers. Chet had wanted this land for a long time, and she doubted that would have changed just because she showed up.

As they bumped along the gravel road that led back up toward the house, Mackenzie watched the familiar landscape roll by. Out the left, low hills rolled out toward the horizon, cut off by a strip of trees. If memory served, those trees lined a creek that meandered through the pasture, complete with a swimming hole and a rope swing. To the right was the Grangers' land, a wooden fence slicing between the properties. The place looked different now that it was hers, though. She felt as if she had to memorize it, figure it out, protect it from a Granger takeover.

When Andy told her about Chet's dislike of her, that he thought that she wasn't the kind of woman who would fit in with them, she'd been doubly hurt. Not only had her father lied to her face for years, but now Chet had been hiding his own bias. She'd never suspected that he felt that way in the few conversations they'd had, and she certainly didn't deserve it. So now that she was the sole owner of this ranch, she couldn't help but feel wary of other people's devious intentions, Chet's included. She'd be responsible for all of this, and that weighed rather heavily on her shoulders.

But this was better than her life in the city had been. What with all of her friends having left for other more exciting opportunities and working a job she truly loathed, even if it did pay moderately well, being responsible for something of this magnitude woke her up in a way she'd never experienced before, not even when visiting here. This was going to be hard—really hard—and somehow she knew it could also be worth it.

"So what happened between Andy and his fiancée?" Mackenzie asked. She'd been wondering what the details were ever since Chet had mentioned it when he arrived.

Chet shrugged. "I don't know too much, but if I had to guess, I'd say it was Andy's fault."

Mackenzie chuckled at his bluntness. "What makes you so sure?"

"Ida's great." Chet glanced in her direction, one arm out the open window, drumming an absent rhythm on the side of the truck. "She's good for him. She settles him down and makes him think. Ida isn't the difficult type. And I know my brother. If there's friction, it's not because of Ida."

The difficult type. Was that what Chet thought of her? And she absolutely could be, especially if he tried to manipulate her out of her ranch. Still, Mackenzie found herself feeling a tiny bit envious. Maybe Andy hadn't been the right guy for her, but Ida had managed to earn Chet's respect, and Chet wasn't easily charmed. Granny had been the same way. She'd been hard to impress, but when she liked someone, that meant something. Perhaps Ida was just a better fit for the family in Chet's eyes than Mack had been.

Difficult. She suppressed the urge to roll her eyes.

Chet looked grim as he drove, the tall, lanky bulk of him filling up that side of the truck. He smelled like hay and hard work, and she realized there were some issues between the brothers that Chet wasn't eager to talk about.

"You and Andy always were pitted against each other," Mackenzie said. She'd meant it as a joke, wanting to defuse the tension, but Chet didn't even crack a smile.

"We're just different." He said the words low enough that she wasn't entirely sure that they were meant for her. "Look, I should probably warn you. There's a developer sniffing around, looking for land to buy up."

"Oh." Mackenzie raised an eyebrow, caught off guard by the sudden declaration. "Granny would have hated that."

"Yeah." The tension in his shoulders eased. "It's not good for Hope. I just wanted you to know so that you could think it through before someone starts trying to sweet-talk you into a sale."

How much were they offering, exactly? She had to admit she was curious. But the old guilt welled up inside her again. This was Granny's ranch, and Granny hadn't left it to her to sell it—of that, she was absolutely certain. Granny had loved this land. She would have known that if she'd left it to Mack's father, he would have sold it without once setting foot on it again. Maybe that was part of why Granny had willed it to Mackenzie, in a hope that someone would love this place as she had.

Chet brought the truck to a stop in front of the house and put it into Park. "I care about this place. If that developer is successful and manages to buy up land around here, it would change Hope…take away some of the heart here. We've got to keep them out."

"I can see that," she agreed. She noticed that he hadn't mentioned her selling to him yet. Maybe he was timing this, gauging her willingness to sell before he made his offer. "Thanks for letting me know."

They were silent for a couple of beats, and she could tell he was still brooding about something.

"And if you could just be careful around Andy—"

"Careful?" She laughed. "Why?"

"Because he dropped himself on my doorstep last night, whining about the woman who was two months away from marrying him, and I don't want to give him any ideas. I have every intention of sending him back home to Ida ASAP."

Mackenzie frowned. What was Chet more worried about—the big developers or his brother's broken engagement?

"What ideas, exactly?"

"Ideas about you." The statement was loaded, and after he'd said it, silence and implication stretched between them. Andy was barely single again, and Chet thought she'd swoop in and scoop him up? It was insulting.

"Is that what you think of me?" she demanded.

"Excuse me?"

"You think I'm back here looking for romance?" Anger bubbled up within her. A woman inherited four hundred acres of Montana ranch land, and he thought she'd wander off after Andy Granger? "I'm here to run a ranch, and you and Andy can work out your family issues on your own. You and Ida can rest easy, Chet. I have no intention of selling out to some faceless corporation, and I have no intention of starting up with Andy again, either."

"That's good."

Mackenzie wanted to reach out and smack this man, but instead she shook her head and smiled coldly.

"I think I'll take care of my own blisters," she said, hopping out of the truck.

"Wait—you're mad?" Chet asked incredulously, leaning down and looking out the open truck window at her. "What just happened here?"

Just like a man, Chet had missed everything between the lines, and Mack turned back toward him in anger.

"I'm a grown woman, Chet. I'm college educated, and I'm the sole owner of four hundred acres. I'm no longer seventeen, and while this might shock you, I don't need a man. I'm also not stupid. So you can stop standing guard and—"

Chet opened the truck door and slammed it shut harder than necessary. He leaned back into the open window and pinned her with an annoyed glare. "I'm not standing guard."

He stalked around the vehicle and up the back stairs to her house.

"Where are you going?" she demanded.

"I'm helping you with those blisters," he retorted, turning flashing gray eyes onto her. "This is ranching lesson number one—you need people. You can never do this on your own. You're going to need neighbors and you're going to need to pitch in to help them, too, because one of these days, you're going to get the flu, or you're going to get your tractor stuck in the mud, or you're going to lose cows through a broken fence... The potential emergencies are pretty much countless. So get off your high horse, get into that house and let me help you sort out your blisters, or tomorrow you're going to be bleeding through your gloves!"

Mack stared at him, stunned. Without another word, he disappeared into the house, leaving Mackenzie outside. She had two choices—go in there and let him help her, or stomp off to the barn or somewhere and make some elaborate point about her independence. She looked down at her hands—they hurt. A little bit of nursing would be nice, she had to admit, so she blew out a sigh and headed into the house.

Chet seemed to know his way around well enough, his boots thunking against the kitchen floor as he paced about, gathering his supplies. He wrenched open a cupboard above the fridge and pulled out a first-aid kit. So that was where Granny had kept it. Good to know.

"Wash up," he said and marched down the hall, his footsteps echoing from the bathroom. She did as he told her—not that she wouldn't have washed her hands, she mentally noted with an eye roll. Then he came back, a bottle of hydrogen peroxide in hand. He deposited everything onto the table and pulled out a chair.

"Sit."

"You're a bossy one," she said with a slight smile.

"Like you wouldn't believe." He pointed to the chair. "I said sit."

Mackenzie gave him an arch look, then complied. He sat in the chair next to her and took her closer hand in his. He pressed his knees together and laid her open hand against the warm valley between them.

"These blisters are too big," he said. "I'll pop the ones that haven't already with a needle, and after they've drained, we'll disinfect it all and let it dry out."

"That's the secret?" she said.

"Yup." He set to work, his hands moving more gently than she'd have thought possible. He pulled out a needle, and she looked away. Thank goodness he finished the job quickly enough. Her hands were still tender, but they'd heal up. She wasn't the first person on the planet to get a blister, and she felt a little ridiculous getting this kind of attention for something so ordinary.

When he was through, Chet stood back up again.

"You'll be fine," he said. "But do me a favor and wait for me before evening chores tonight. You're going to have to build up to this kind of work, and there's no way around that."

She could see that he was right, and she nodded mutely.

"And one more thing." He pulled open the door and looked back at her, gray eyes boring into hers. "I wasn't suggesting that you'd take advantage of Andy. I was saying that he's not completely over you. Just...be careful."

Andy was the boy who'd unceremoniously dumped her...the boy she'd always wondered about in spite of herself. He'd been her first big heartbreak, the one she'd always fantasized about running into when she looked fantastic and successful. And Chet was saying that he still had feelings for her?

Chet didn't mention anything further, and she didn't ask. He simply stepped outside, slamming the door behind him. She went to the window and watched him stride away from the house, hop up into his truck and drive off without so much as a backward glance.

She looked down at her newly bandaged hands. Chet had a point about needing neighbors. She couldn't be responsible for even fifteen cows without someone else to lean on if the worst should happen. And it looked as if Chet wasn't going to let her be choosy about whom she chose to lean on, either.

Chapter 3

After a sunny morning, clouds had been rolling in all afternoon, sweeping across the landscape but so far leaving them without any rain. Montana needed the moisture, and like every other landholder in these parts, Chet had been watching the sky, hoping for more than an overcast day. This evening, he stood by the back door of Mackenzie's barn as the cows filed inside, hooves plodding hollowly against concrete, and watched as Mackenzie closed them into their stalls.

He'd never seen Mack as much of a rancher in their youth. She'd always been the city girl visiting her grandmother's ranch, but the past decade had changed a lot. Her teenage spunk had matured into a stubborn fortitude. The accidental flirtation that she'd never seemed entirely aware of had evaporated. She now seemed to know what she could make a man feel and her appropriate reserve made him only all the more drawn to her. She knew what she had to offer, and she wasn't playing games. All of that potential had blossomed. If he'd been smitten back then, he knew that he could fall even harder now if he wasn't careful.

The goats came in after the cows, and Butter Cream ambled in last of all, her belly less full and a tiny white kid in tow. Chet hadn't seen the kid when they'd opened the pasture gates. It looked as if Butter Cream had taken care of things herself—a week early, at that. The baby was mussed up from having been licked by its mother, and Chet crouched down to do a quick sex check. The kid was a buck, and its belly was full of milk—an excellent sign. Butter Cream was an experienced mother, and she knew how to care for a kid without much intervention. She'd had only singletons in the past, though.

"She had her baby!" Mackenzie exclaimed, and she bent down, holding her fingers out toward them. Butter Cream let her approach, and the baby stretched to give her a curious sniff. "I guess you were wrong," Mack said. "There's only one."

"I'm not wrong." It was possible that the second baby was still inside and Butter Cream might need some help to deliver, but there was most definitely a second baby.

"Let me see…" Chet came closer. He and Butter Cream had a good relationship going, and she allowed him to feel her belly. It was still distended from pregnancy, but it was empty of babies. That meant there was at least one more kid outside in the field without its mother.

"What's wrong?" Mack asked. "Is she going to have another one?"

"She already had it," Chet replied. "And it's out there somewhere."

He jutted his chin toward the open barn door, and a gust of cold, damp air swept inside at the same moment, raising goose bumps on her arms.

"How do you know?" She rubbed her arms, her gaze flickering toward the door.

"I told you that she was pregnant with more than one. The other might not have survived, but there are times when a goat will accept one twin and reject the other. If it's alive, it won't be for long if we don't find it."

Mackenzie sobered and stood up instantly. "Come on, girl," she said gently, herding Butter Cream toward the stall. "In your pen. Let's go…"

When they reached the door, the wind was whipping through the long grass in ripples and sending up spirals of dust from the dirt road.

"Where would it be?" Mack asked, raising her voice above the sound of the wind, and she stopped to look around, holding her hat down with one hand.

"They were in the small pasture, right?" Chet asked. "The one beside the cows?"

Mack squinted, suddenly looking less sure of herself. "I think so."

"Come on." He headed for the truck. "We'll drive over. It'll be faster. But when we get there, we'll have to search on foot."

Mackenzie beat him to the truck, and by the time she slid into the driver's seat, the first few fat drops of rain were hitting the dusty gravel like tiny bombs. The air smelled moist and good, but rain also meant that the lost kid was going to be even colder than it already was. He could only hope that Butter Cream had cleaned the baby off before abandoning it.

The truck lurched forward before Chet had even slammed the door shut, and Mackenzie glanced in his direction, then back at the road. The wind was blowing harder now, and the rain started to fall in earnest, hurtling straight into the windshield and blurring their vision, even with the wipers sloshing back and forth at full speed.

"I can barely see!" Mack said.

"There, there—" Chet pointed to the turn that would bring them to the smallest enclosed pasture, which was also closest to the barn, and she hauled the wheel left, the tires spinning in the newly created mud. As they pulled up to the gate, the truck dropped heavily at the front end, and the tires spun.

"What was that?" Mack exclaimed, leaning forward to look.

"Pothole. See if you can back up," Chet suggested.

Mack put the truck into Reverse and hit the gas, but it made no difference. The tires spun again, but they weren't going anywhere.

"Shoot…" Mack heaved a sigh, and for a moment, he thought he saw tears mist her eyes. He knew she wasn't looking for sympathy, but he had the urge to put an arm around her—an urge he quickly quashed.

"Come on," Chet said. "Let's go look for the kid, and we'll figure out the truck when we find it. I have some tricks up my sleeve yet."

She sucked in a breath and exchanged a look with him. Then they both pushed their hats more firmly onto their heads and pushed open their doors, hopping out into the hammering rain. Chet wasn't sure what he expected of Mack out here, but she wasn't waiting on him and beelined into the middle of the pasture. Chet stayed closer to the fence. They'd cover more ground searching different areas.

He was still frustrated, though. Ten years had passed and some things just didn't change. Last night, Andy had called dibs—even though he didn't know that Mack was back yet—and while that was a stupid way to decide any-thing, his younger brother also held all the cards. Chet shaded his eyes and looked toward Mackenzie, who was standing with her back to him, legs akimbo and hand still holding her hat securely on her head. She was somehow both softer and stronger at the same time. She'd got-ten only more beautiful over the years.

A faint bleat caught his ear, and he nearly stepped on the tiny thing before he saw it. The kid was drenched with rain, even smaller than its brother back in the barn. It was chocolate brown and lay curled up in a pathetic little ball by a fence post.

"Over here!" Chet hollered, and Mack jogged toward them. The rain had wet her through, her shirt clinging to her body and rivulets of water pouring down her collarbones and sticking her hair into dark gold tendrils against her skin. Chet picked up the goat and it shivered in his arms.

"It's alive—that's a relief," Mack said, wiping water from her face. "I think I saw an old blanket in the back of the truck—"

"Helen always kept one back there," Chet said. "If Butter Cream won't take her, you might just have earned yourself a bottle baby."

Mack gave him an appropriate look of alarm. At least she could appreciate how much work was coming her way. They trudged back through the blinding rain toward the truck. The vehicle hung at an angle, the front driver's-side wheel deep in a pothole. She stayed close to his side, the warmth of her body emanating against his arm, and when he looked down at her, he realized that Mack was oddly comforting—a comfort he hadn't known he'd even needed.

Chet pulled open the passenger's-side door, and between them both, they got the tiny goat wrapped in the blanket. It needed milk, and they didn't have much time before it lost its strength, and that would be fatal.

"Go around and put it in Reverse," Chet said, pulling Mack clear of another pothole as he spoke. She leaned into him as he tugged her to the side, her slight weight colliding with his chest. "Easy does it," he said, boosting her back up. He didn't dare let his mind go to the possibilities of her in his arms.

Mack met his gaze and a smile crinkled at the corners of her eyes. Just as quickly, she was out of his arms, and she hurried around the back of the truck to hop into the driver's side. The rain came down in a steady sheet, and Chet was pretty sure that there wasn't a part of him that was dry at this point, but it would be a while before he was back home, so it was better not to think about it.

Chet levered his body against the grate of the truck and shouted, "Now!"

The wheel started to spin and he pushed against the grate with all his strength. His boots slid in the mud, and he could hear the tires tearing into the side of the pothole. When it stopped, the truck sank even farther down. This wasn't going to work.

Chet stood up and went around to the window.

"It's no good," Chet said. "We're only digging deeper."

Mackenzie locked eyes with him for a moment, then nodded. She reached for the bundled-up little goat and cuddled it close against her chest.

"I guess we'd better walk, then," she said. "What'll I do about the truck?"

He took her by the arm, helping to lift her back down to the ground. She bent her head against the rain, and he slammed the door shut behind them.

"This is why you have neighbors," he said, raising his voice above the drum of the storm. "Andy and I used to get our truck out of potholes all the time. I just need some twine and a two-by-four. But first things first."

They picked up their pace, rushing through the slanting rain toward the blurred shape of the barn. The road was slick with mud, and at one point, Mackenzie slipped, falling heavily against him. He caught her and kept a solid arm around her waist after that. She felt good in his arms—warm and slippery and soft. He wasn't supposed to even entertain thoughts like these right now. He had bigger issues— like holding what was left of the Granger family together and not losing his ranch, both of which he'd fail at if he let his attraction to Mackenzie get in the way. Mack was a distraction he couldn't actually afford.

"You were right about neighbors, Chet," she said as they finally made it to the barn and ducked under the eaves. "I have no idea what I'd have done without you. I suppose I owe you one."

She was so close to him that he could feel her breath and the way she shivered. She looked down at the tiny kid in her arms, and he was tempted to put his arms around her and warm her up, but he couldn't guarantee that he'd stop there, so instead, he shot her a grin and said, "We'll figure it out."

A few ideas—none of which were appropriate—flitted through his mind, but he shoved them back. The more prominent thought right now was that he couldn't get her truck out of that ditch without another body, and he knew exactly who he'd need to call. He ran his ranch on a skeleton crew—money being tight lately—and his own workers were tending to his herds right now. That left one person with nothing at all to do except sit around Chet's house and feel sorry for himself...

He'd been hoping to keep Mack to himself for a little longer, but it looked as though he'd have to haul Andy out here and share some of that glory.

Blast.

Mackenzie sat cross-legged inside Butter Cream's stall, holding the tiny brown goat up to the mother's teat. Butter Cream stepped away every time the kid's little mouth made contact.

"Butter Cream, this is your baby," she said firmly. "Come on now."

She offered some hay for Butter Cream to eat out of her hands, but the goat sidled away again as the tiny kid tried to latch on. Mackenzie felt tears of frustration rising. The baby was hungry and bleated plaintively, a weak, wavering cry. She guided the kid's head forward once more, and the barn door banged open, making Butter Cream startle and stumble forward, stepping heavily on Mackenzie's hand.

"Ouch!"

Chet came inside, and behind him came his brother. She couldn't get a clear look at Andy, who was the smaller man of the two, and she caught her heart speeding up. She hadn't seen or heard from Andy Granger since the day he broke up with her, though she'd gone over what she'd say to him a hundred times if she ever got the chance. And here it was.

When Andy finally came up to his brother's side, she was surprised to see that he'd changed quite a bit. He was still several inches shorter than Chet, but the years had made more of a man of him. His physique was still fit, although broader now that he was fully grown, and his red hair had darkened into something closer to auburn with a few strands of silver. Andy glanced around nervously, and when his gaze fell on her, he gave her a tentative smile.

"Mackenzie Vaughn," he said, his voice low and warm. "Is it ever good to see you."

She hadn't expected that, and she pushed herself to her feet. "Hi, Andy."

"It's been a while." Andy came up to Butter Cream's stall, and Mackenzie opened the door, letting herself out.

"A long while," she agreed.

Andy leaned in to give her a hug just as she was about to move away toward the barn sink, and they had an awkward collision and a back pat. Andy laughed uncomfortably.

"Sorry—should have warned you," he said.

"It's okay. I was going to—"

"Yeah, yeah."

This couldn't have gone worse, even in her most vivid imagination. In her mind, she'd always given him some searing comment about his inability to appreciate a good woman, but she couldn't pull one together for the life of her. And suddenly it didn't seem to matter so much.

"Chet, I think I'm going to have a bottle baby on my hands." She turned to the older brother, who stood behind Andy with his arms crossed over his broad chest. His gray eyes were focused on her, and she felt a blush rise in her cheeks.

"I'll get you a sterilized pail to start milking," Chet said, and he tossed her a small teasing smile. He knew exactly how awkward this was.

"I can get that," Andy said, his old charming smile coming back. "If you tell me where it is, I guess…"

"I'll get it." Chet cast his brother a flat look and strode off toward the back of the barn.

"So…" Andy said, once his brother was out of earshot. "I hear you inherited this place."

"I hear you got engaged," she countered.

"I did." Andy laughed softly. "Unfortunately, we just broke up."

Shaky relationships were Mackenzie's forte,

and she gave him a sympathetic smile. "I'm sorry about that."

Andy shrugged. "We were together four years, so it's complicated."

"I imagine." Somehow, when she'd pictured this scene over the years, she'd never included all of their respective baggage in the picture. This wasn't about proving a point anymore.

"How are your parents?" Andy asked after a few beats of silence.

"Still driving me nuts." She smiled wryly. "Dad should have inherited this place. Not me."

"Is he mad?"

She shrugged. "Hurt, I guess…okay, and mad. Not at me. More at the situation. It looks like Granny held a grudge."

They exchanged a look. Andy had known all about her father's dalliances. He'd been her boyfriend during her parents' divorce, which meant he'd heard all the unsavory details already. It was strangely comfortable to be able to skip all the explanations.

"So you've been living in Billings, too?" Andy asked.

"Yep. That's where both my parents are, and the rest of the family, so…"

"If I'd known you were around…" He

cleared his throat. "I've been managing that big Ford dealership on the west end. You should stop by sometime."

"Well, it's a bit of a drive now," she pointed out, and Andy laughed.

"Yeah, well... I guess we're neighbors again, aren't we?"

Chet came back at that moment and handed her a bucket. Andy fell silent, and she could feel the tension between the brothers. That was something that hadn't changed a bit. Chet grinned at her. "Do you know how to milk a goat?"

"No," she admitted. "I'll need a quick lesson."

Chet nudged past his brother, and Andy looked less than willing to give room—or was that her imagination? He didn't have a lot of choice, though. Chet was bigger and more solidly muscled, and he pulled open the stall gate for her to go back in. Chet followed her, and Andy leaned over the top rail, watching them. It almost felt like old times, the three of them in the barn together, except in the past decade all three of them had inherited land, one had gotten himself engaged and life had become a whole lot more complicated. Their parents' worries were now their own.

"Okay, so you have to grab ahold like this and then squeeze downward, like you're emptying a tube of toothpaste." Chet demonstrated, and a hiss of milk shot into the bucket. "Your turn."

Mackenzie leaned over, her arms pressing against the hard muscle in Chet's. She managed a few squirts into the bucket and she felt a surge of victory. After a day like today, she needed to win at something, and if that was milking a goat, she'd take it.

"Look at you," Andy said from where he watched. "I never thought I'd see you working a ranch, Mack. Remember how we used to go into town just before chores?"

Andy laughed and Chet raised an eyebrow at Mack questioningly. On this side of things, her teenaged antics that had pulled Andy away from his chores seemed stupid.

"Sorry," she said softly. "It seemed fun at the time…"

"It *was* fun," Andy insisted. "We used to play pool, remember?"

Andy was trying to pull her into old memories, but the memories he'd held on to weren't the same ones she had. He remembered ducking out on chores. She remembered holding hands in the hayloft. Chet pushed himself to his feet and stepped away, the place where his arm had been pressed against hers suddenly cold. Mackenzie glanced up at Andy.

"A lot's changed," she said, feeling almost as if she had to apologize to him for that. She couldn't even explain everything she meant by those words, but obviously she was no longer the teenager who enjoyed bucking off responsibility.

"Speaking of change…" Andy turned toward Chet and took a few steps away. The milk continued to hiss into the bucket as Mackenzie worked, but she could still make out the men talking. "The whole family ranch business is in the past, Chet. You know it."

"Since when?" Chet demanded.

"Since the big beef suppliers started taking over. You make pennies on the dollar out here. You work yourself to death." There was a pause, and Mackenzie focused on the rhythmic movement of her fingers. "Tell him I'm right, Mack."

"Leave her out of this," Chet growled.

"She can have an opinion," Andy retorted. "What do you think, Mack?"

Mackenzie rested the side of her head against the goat's back. She wasn't about to get in the middle of a Granger brother squabble. "I'm pretty new to this, Andy, so you'll have to leave me out of your debates."

"But you can see where the future's headed, am I right?" Andy pressed. When Mack didn't answer, he sighed. "Chet, you love this life, but I can't do it. It's not for me."

Mackenzie looked back at the two brothers. Andy's back was to her, but she could clearly see Chet's face, and his light eyes flashed with suppressed anger. There was something else going on here, something a whole lot deeper than personal preferences, and Andy's comment had the sound of a declaration.

Andy's voice lowered. "I need to liquidate. You have to understand that."

They stepped farther away and she could no longer make out their words over the sound of the milk driving into the bucket. The Granger brothers had always been at the opposite ends of pretty much any debate. You name it, they'd quarrel over it. Today, though, the stakes seemed higher—she could tell, if only by looking at the expression on Chet's face.

The shrill ring of a cell phone broke through the hum of barn sounds, and Andy walked away, picking up the call. Chet wandered back toward Mackenzie.

"What's going on?" she asked.

"It's okay—it's nothing."

His gray eyes had turned a brooding charcoal, and he leaned over the rail, his gaze directed inward.

"You own your ranch, right?" she asked cautiously.

"I own half of it," he said, his eyes flickering to his brother again, and suddenly it made sense to her.

"And Andy owns the other half," she concluded. "So when he said he had to liquidate—"

Chet cast her a dark look. "Yeah. It's complicated."

Complicated. That was the word of the day, it seemed.

"That's how Andy described his relationship with Ida," she observed.

"Well, we're all a bit complicated, aren't we?" Chet said, his tone bitter. "Andy has the pleasure of being as complicated as he likes, and the rest of us just have to roll with it."

"The developers?" she clarified.

"If he doesn't change his mind." Chet scuffed his boot across the cement floor.

"Buy him out," she suggested.

"He won't sell to me." Chet turned and met her gaze, and she realized with a sinking in her gut that the very permanence of the land out here wasn't quite as strong as one might like. Was it possible that the Grangers would sell and she'd be left out here in Hope, alone, trying to forge her own ties and help lines without them?

Chet handed her a white screw-top bottle with a goat-sized nipple on top. She didn't need instructions on how to put all the parts together for this, and she lifted the bucket away from Butter Cream's hooves and poured a stream of creamy froth into the bottle, spilling a little onto the ground between her boots. The other kid moved in to nurse immediately, and Mackenzie shifted aside to give them space, and there was the sound of hungry slurping. She twisted the nipple onto the bottle.

"Here." Chet came back into the stall and picked up the brown kid. It kicked its hooves a few times, but Chet got the tiny creature expertly tucked up in his arms.

"Here's your meal, baby," Mackenzie crooned, and she eased the nipple into the kid's mouth. It pulled back in confusion at the rubber, but after a few more tries, the little thing got the hang of it and started to drink hungrily, milk drenching its chin.

"You've got your work cut out for you now," Andy said, sauntering back over.

"Looks like," Mackenzie agreed with a smile. "How often will she need a bottle?"

"Every four hours for a bit," Chet said. "Set your alarm."

Mackenzie smiled wanly. It looked as though she wouldn't be sleeping much for the next little while.

Andy's phone rang again, and he picked it up with a curt "Yeah?" Then his tone softened. "Hey, Ida… Yeah, I'm just out in the barn with Chet." He paused. "Yeah, yeah… I know. It'll be another couple of weeks before I can get some movers, but I'll give you plenty of warning before they come…"

Mackenzie glanced up at Chet and they exchanged a silent look. This was Andy's ex, and the sadness in his voice was unmistakable. She'd known that Andy would love again after her—obviously, since he'd been the one to end it—but listening to Andy talk like that to another woman twisted something inside her.

"It must be hard to try to unravel a life together," Mack said quietly.

They weren't the same three teens who used to hang out. Ten years had changed them all.

"True enough," Chet said. "Ida's just about family now. So it'll be hard on a lot of people."

"So the family really likes her, huh?" she said.

"Yeah."

The confirmation stung. They really liked Ida, but none of the Grangers had approved of her. Least of all Chet.

"And you want them back together," she said, attempting a little levity in her tone despite the disappointment in her gut.

"Well, you know me. Family first," Chet said, his voice a low rumble in his chest.

Family first. That was what Chet Granger had always stood for. Most of the time, Mack would agree with that sentiment, but there were times that she wished he'd just choke on it.

Chapter 4

The next afternoon, after Mackenzie had given Chocolate Truffle her bottle of milk—she'd named the little goat during one of the nighttime feeds—she leaned back against the fence and let her eyes close. She'd been up three times the night before to feed the baby goat, and she realized that if she'd adjusted that feeding schedule, it could have been one trip out to the barn in the moonlight, nightgown flapping against the tops of her gum boots. The other two feeds could have been done just before bed and then at sunrise.

"Oh, I feel stupid…" she murmured to herself. She felt like a first-time parent who was too tired to connect the dots. She'd never roll her eyes at her friends complaining about lack of sleep again. This job was much harder than she'd ever anticipated, and if she was serious about keeping this ranch, she'd soon need to hire some help. Could getting up at night to bottle-feed a goat be in someone else's job description?

So far today, she'd mucked out the barn, cleaned the chicken coop, temporarily fixed a rotting fence rail, started sorting through her grandmother's garage and harvested some zucchini that had gotten too big. Whether or not they'd still be edible, she wasn't sure. What she was certain of was her exhaustion.

She opened her eyes again, enjoying the warmth of the sunlight as it soaked into her jeans, warming her legs and arms deliciously. Chocolate Truffle stood a few feet away, her little tail wagging back and forth cheerfully. A full tummy made for a happy kid, it seemed. Mackenzie glanced around in time to see Butter Cream and her second twin trotting blithely across the field, toward Chet's barn.

"Oh, for crying out loud!" she muttered, pushing herself to her feet. Then she raised her voice. "Butter Cream, get back here!"

Mackenzie had left Butter Cream in the barn

today so that she would be undisturbed with her new babies. She was still hoping that the mama goat would accept her abandoned kid—perhaps that wasn't realistic, but a woman could try. Mackenzie wasn't sure what she expected when she shouted after Butter Cream, but the goat stoically ignored her and continued on its journey to the preferred barn. She looked down at the tiny brown goat who stayed by her side.

"You seem to like me, at least," she said wryly. "Come on. I'll bring you back to the barn…"

How could one goat and two kids be this much trouble? She scooped up Chocolate Truffle into her arms and the kid let out a low bleat of contentment. Mackenzie was the source of milk, and this little goat knew where her bread was buttered. It didn't take long to get her resettled in the stall with some fresh hay, and Mackenzie ventured back outside into the sun to go fetch Butter Cream.

The goat had already disappeared by the time Mackenzie ducked through the rails of the fence and headed in the direction of Chet's barn. Across the stretch of land and down a rolling grass-covered incline, she could see the cows' pasture. Her small herd stood in bovine bliss, tails flicking flies away and jaws munching in slow grinding revolutions. The intermittent lowing of the cattle surfed along the sweet breeze, and she paused for a moment, soaking up the beauty of it all.

Comparing this—tired as she was—to long hours in a fluorescent-lit cubicle was almost painful. This was the kind of scene she used to dream about while sitting in front of her computer screen and wishing the time would pass faster. Keeping that cubicle job as long as she had was one of her major regrets. She'd kept working at the insurance agency for a number of reasons—namely that it paid fairly well and that she wasn't sure what else she was qualified to do. Looking back on it, there had to have been something—anything, really—that would have been better, but she'd stayed put because she was afraid of change.

When she'd quit that job, her work friends had thrown her a little party with a store-bought cake and some paper plates. They'd all wished her well, signed a card and gone back to their desks after chatting for an hour in the break room. The hole she'd left would be filled promptly, and before a month was out, she was sure that they'd have forgotten her. So why had she been so loyal to a job she was so indifferent toward? Had a paycheck really made her fluorescent-lit days worth it?

"It was dumb," she muttered to herself. She'd never make the mistake of staying in a rut again.

Mackenzie continued toward Chet's barn, but she paused as she saw Chet strolling her way, Butter Cream following as obediently as a lamb and her little white buckling tucked under Chet's muscular arm. Her heart sped up a little at the sight of him, and she realized that she was relieved to see him. Quietly, over the past few days, Chet had become a part of her routine. Somehow, his dry humor and his comfortable silences gave her something calm and reassuring to look forward to.

"Morning." He tipped his hat with the other hand, and he slowed as he approached her. His light gaze found hers and a smile turned up the corners of his lips.

"I was just coming for them." She returned his smile, then nodded down at Butter Cream. "Why won't you just take this goat off my hands, Chet?"

"I told you before," he said. "I don't need a goat."

Mackenzie couldn't help the laugh that bubbled up from her throat, and she turned around and started back toward her property, but she could feel Chet's strong presence close behind her. He caught up and matched her stride, his arm inches from hers.

"Somehow, I expected nothing less," she said. "Have you always been this stubborn?"

"You tell me."

The Chet from a decade ago had been quiet and brooding, too, but he had nothing on the man beside her. Chet today was solid, resolute, and he wasn't brooding so much as determined. She had a feeling that once he'd made his mind up about something, there would be no turning him. That was both frustrating and reassuring. Chet Granger was who he was, and you could take him or leave him.

"Far as I can tell." She eyed him sideways. "So what do you do for fun around here?"

"This isn't fun?" he asked drily.

"That's not what I'm talking about and you know it," she shot back. "What I remember of you, you were always knee-deep in muck or riding off into the sunset."

"Sounds about right," he replied. "That's why you chose Andy instead."

There was something deep in his tone that made her heart rate quicken. Was he suggesting something about all those years ago? It was true—Andy had worked significantly less than his older brother. Except where she was concerned—he'd worked hard to win her. He'd take the time to come find her, take her to town for a cone at Beauty's Ice Cream or for a walk down Main Street to look at the murals painted on the sides of the buildings depicting old farming techniques from the nineteenth century. Andy had pursued.

"I don't remember you being interested," she retorted.

"Don't you?" His tone lowered and his eyes held hers for a moment in a way that made her breath catch in her throat.

"I don't," she said with a short laugh. "You were so reserved."

And she would have noticed if he'd returned her crush. She'd watched for it, wondering if he liked her at all, but he hadn't shown interest.

"You were taken."

His words took her by surprise. Had there been more underneath that stern reserve, or was she misunderstanding the meaning behind those words?

"So you—" she started.

"It was a long time ago, and like you pointed out, I wasn't much fun." He gave a rueful smile.

Mackenzie swallowed, his words still circling her mind. He'd felt something for her back then…and that knowledge warmed her. She'd been so certain that he hadn't…but that didn't explain why he'd tell Andy to dump her. Was it from juvenile jealousy, or had his attraction to her been only that—attraction and nothing that could last?

"So what do *you* do when you aren't working?" he asked, seeming to be done with discussing his own feelings.

"I used to take vacations. Travel."

"Yeah?" Chet shot her a curious look. "Where've you been?"

"I've been to France, Germany, Mexico, Alaska and Hawaii. I like planning trips. How about you?"

"I went to Colorado once for a buddy's wedding," he said. Mack waited for him to continue, and when he didn't, she smiled cautiously.

"That's it?"

"I stay busy around here."

"And you never feel the urge to just get away?" she pressed.

"Not really."

"We should take care of that," she said with a quick laugh. And she wasn't entirely joking, either. It dawned on her that she'd like to spend more time with Chet…maybe introduce him to something new, too. "Chet Granger, you are far too serious. Do you realize that?"

"So I've been told."

"It can't be all work, Chet."

"It isn't." He glanced at her, and the intensity in his expression made her mind run in less appropriate directions. What would Chet be like when he was focused on something other than the ranch? What would Chet be like focused on her?

"No?" She tried to will the color out of her cheeks.

"I also read."

Mackenzie blinked, then sobered. "What kinds of books?"

"Anything and everything," he replied. "History, philosophy, biographies—"

"And you'd rather read than get out there and see something different?" she pressed.

Chet was silent for a moment. "Let's put it this way," he said quietly. "Standing on the ground of a different country doesn't do as much for me as sending down my roots right here."

"Oh." Mack felt the weight in his words, and her joking seemed out of place now. "I think Granny was that way, too."

"Doesn't mean you can't travel," he said. "You just need some reliable ranch hands, is all."

They were nearing her barn, and Chet looked at her again, those gray eyes lingering on her face for a moment before he turned away.

She'd lived for her vacations these past several years, and she'd made enough that she'd been able to go somewhere fantastic every summer. The getting away had been the point— getting away from work, her parents and the humdrum of Billings. Would she feel the same way about this ranch after a few months, that desperate need to escape it all? Or was there something to those roots that Chet talked about? She had to admit that it was appealing.

Mackenzie pulled on the barn door and it slid open on its rail. Butter Cream waited patiently until Chet put the tiny kid down and then trotted into her stall, where her little brown doeling waited, curled into a ball in a bed of hay. Mack closed up the stall, and they walked back outside.

"So how are things with Andy?" she asked.

Chet shrugged. "Andy's the same as always."

Mack wasn't entirely sure what he meant by that, and she eyed him inquiringly. "I wonder why he came here." Chet stayed silent, his gaze traveling along the fence line, but he didn't move away from her, so she continued. "I mean, his life is in Billings, isn't it? You'd think he'd have had a few friends he could have crashed with. Plus, doesn't he make a pretty good living at that car dealership? I'm sure he could have afforded a week or two in a hotel."

Chet glanced toward her, that stony reserve slowly cracking as their eyes locked. "I've always fixed things for Andy. Maybe he came here for me to fix it."

"But why you?" she persisted. "Why does it always fall to you to put things back together?"

He didn't respond for a moment, then shrugged. "If someone breaks down on the side of the road, you've got to stop and help for the simple reason that you're the one who's there. If a neighbor's tractor gets stuck in mud, you're obliged to head on over and lend a hand for the simple reason that you live close by. Both our parents are gone, and while we've got aunts and uncles, it's not the same. Not really. Call it obligation or responsibility, but I'm the one who's left."

A cow lowed from the field, and another answered. A warm breeze whisked across the open land, flattening her shirt against her side.

She was rolling his words around in her mind when he added, "You're going to need some salt licks." His tone was unchanged, and she squinted at him, slightly confused.

"Excuse me?"

"You need salt licks. There are only a few left in the storeroom. I'm going to town. Do you want to come along and see the ranch-supply store? It's your go-to for pretty much anything you're going to need from this point on."

"Yes." She nodded. "Thanks. That would be great."

Granny had taken her to the supply store a couple of times that she could remember, but she'd need to be reacquainted with the place, obviously.

"Okay, then." He resettled his hat on his head. "I'll come by and pick you up in about an hour. I have a few things to finish up first."

"Sure."

He nodded a goodbye, then headed out across that stretch of grass again toward his own barn. He moved with ease, his shoulders swaying as he walked. It was as though none of this could change him, and he remained as constant as the rough prairie grass. As exasperating as he was, it was comforting in a way, but one worry nagged the back of her mind.

Why was Chet doing all of this for *her*? She didn't want to be the obligation next door—the stuck tractor, the broken-down vehicle that he was duty bound to help.

"Chet!" she called, and he turned back.

"Yeah?"

"Are you doing all this because you feel obliged?"

"Nope," he replied, and a grin split his face. "I'm doing it 'cause you're pretty."

And with that, he turned and continued his walk away from her. Mack felt the blush rise in her cheeks and she smiled in spite of herself. Chet had some charm of his own, hidden away under that gruff, obstinate exterior.

She had an hour. And she also had chickens to check on. Work around here never seemed to stop.

Chet headed across the scrub grass toward his home.

What a stupid line, he chastised himself. *Because she's pretty? Of course she's pretty. She knows that. And it doesn't matter—it shouldn't matter.*

He'd be a much wiser man if he could just resist the urge to answer a few of those questions she cast his way. He was an honest man, but there wouldn't be any harm in just shutting his mouth every so often. He'd been able to do it back when they were all teenagers, so why the sudden urge to start saying what he was thinking?

He resisted the urge to look back. He wasn't supposed to be flirting. This wasn't the plan. Neither was falling for her all over again.

His herds were already grazing for the summer, and the calves had nearly doubled in size since they were born in the spring. They were out of harm's way, and most were grazing alongside their mothers at this point. The crops were in, they weren't set to rotate grazing fields for another few weeks, and now he was changing his focus to getting things organized for the inevitable winter. No matter how bright and cheery a summer day, he was always aware just how fleeting the season was.

Before he left for town, he needed to take another look at the finances to prepare for a meeting with the bank, so he made his way to the house, kicking his boots against the steps to loosen any dirt as he reached the back door.

Inside, there was no sign of Andy, except for a few dirty dishes in the sink. Chet let out a sigh of relief. As much as he wanted to patch things up with his only brother, they irritated each other. They'd always been opposites, but over the past decade, he'd gotten used to his own space. He liked rattling around in this old house, and his brother's shoes in the middle of the doorway or toiletries piled on the bathroom counter were a grating reminder that he wasn't alone.

Chet pulled down the ledger and flipped it open, but his mind wasn't on profits and losses for the past few years or projected earnings for this calendar year. He needed to think about getting a loan large enough to rival the amount the developers were willing to pay his brother, but that kind of money wouldn't be easy to come by, and the very thought of owing that much filled his gut with cement.

And still, he'd invited Mack along for the ride.

What had he been thinking? Only that he wanted to be alone with her for a little while. He liked being in the truck with her when he could smell that soft floral scent of the perfume she sometimes wore. While he didn't want an audience for this meeting with the loan officer, or for the fallout of the meeting, he couldn't think of anyone else he'd rather have near him.

Which was dangerous, because he was pretty confident that she didn't feel the same way.

If Andy sold their pasture, Chet was the one with the most at stake. He needed a plan B, some sort of safety net if his brother did this. There wasn't any pasture for sale for about three hundred miles. If he was forced to buy pasture out that far, his cattle drives would be marathons. Or he could do the unthinkable and sell his land, too. He could buy farther out— maybe in a different county—and start fresh.

The thought was a painful one because this land held him by the heartstrings, and it was right next to the Vaughn ranch... Why was it that Mackenzie's face kept rising up in his mind at the thought of selling? It felt like abandoning her, even though they were nothing more than neighbors. But she needed him and his expertise more than she knew right now. Other guys weren't quite as principled as he was, and they might take advantage. She'd be easy pickings for a bitter ranch hand—cattle rustling could make a significant dent in a ranch's profit. With him next door, she'd be protected. She didn't know that, of course, but it was true.

Chet stood to lose a lot if he sold, but he stood to lose something different if Mackenzie didn't end up keeping the ranch. He'd been in love with her ten years ago, and now he realized those feelings had never really gone away. They'd come back in a flood when he'd clapped eyes on her again. How dumb that was, he wasn't sure. So if either of them sold, he would lose those moments standing at the fence, watching her sweet-talk a goat or giving her a hand with some chore. He would lose the possibility of her tramping out to his barn in search of Butter Cream or the opportunity to sit alone with her in the cab of a pickup truck, bumping down the gravel road that led toward the barn. He would lose all those unknown possibilities that lay in the days ahead—potential moments when she might finally see what she'd never seen in him before.

Chet rubbed his hands over his face. He had to get his head back in the game. His heart couldn't lead this, and he knew that. He glanced at the clock. He had forty minutes now. He sucked in a deep breath and turned his attention to the ledgers in front of him.

One step at a time. He needed this loan.

Chapter 5

When Mackenzie hopped up into the cab of Chet's pickup, he noticed that she'd changed her clothes. She now wore a clean pair of jeans and a pale pink blouse that brought out the blush in her cheeks. Her hair hung loosely down her back in a sun-streaked blond cascade, and as she slid into the seat next to him, he could smell the fresh scent of a citrusy perfume.

"I just gave Chocolate Truffle her bottle," Mackenzie said. "But I'm kind of afraid to leave the property. Do you know what I mean?"

Chet chuckled. "You'll get used to it. Nothing will fall apart."

It was a good sign in his books. She was starting to sense the magnitude of her responsibility. She'd also have to learn how to cut loose from time to time, though, or the stress would do her in.

"Not that I could even stop it," she replied with a wry smile.

"You're getting better at this." He shrugged. "Chasing down goats is part of the job."

"Speaking of goats," she said, "why does Butter Cream love you so much?"

"I'm good-looking." He grinned, then laughed. "Joking. I bottle-fed her as a kid."

"You did?"

"Goats are very loving, and they don't forget their mamas. A lot like cows."

"So Butter Cream sees you as her mama." She gave him a small smile. "Well, as much of a mama as a six-foot-five rancher can be."

"Yeah, you could say that." It didn't matter how manly you were or how many bales you could toss into the back of a truck; if you held a bottle in those callused hands, you were the mother. "Helen didn't have the heart to put Butter Cream down when she was born, and she asked me to help her do it. Butter Cream was an underweight newborn kid that neither of us expected to survive. Her mother had triplets and abandoned her. She was as weak as a kitten, but I didn't have the heart to do it, either. So I bottle-fed her, against my better judgment, and she started to put on weight. So my job was cut out for me."

"So why didn't you keep her?" she asked.

"She was Helen's."

"And Granny didn't offer to give her to you?"

"Okay, maybe she did. But I didn't need a goat."

And that was the truth of it. He knew back then what trouble goats could be, and he ran a ranch, not a hobby farm. He raised cattle for beef, and he didn't want the trouble of goats... but that didn't mean he didn't stop and visit Butter Cream and give her a scratch over the fence. He wasn't made of stone.

Mackenzie rolled her eyes. "You're still a stubborn one, Chet Granger."

This wasn't the first time she'd described him that way, and maybe he was. But a stubborn streak served him well when it came to making a living off the land. Weather didn't always cooperate. Droughts drove up the cost of feeding two hundred and fifty head of cattle. Even dealing with Andy took a fair amount of fortitude. If he weren't the stubborn son of a gun that he was, he wouldn't still be ranching this land. And maybe it would be enough to keep him ranching this land if he just held on long enough.

The trip into Hope took only about fifteen minutes when hitting the gas, and the wheels sent a billow of dust out behind as they approached the highway. He liked this drive. It was straight and there was little traffic along the two-lane highway, oncoming traffic separated by a faded yellow dash.

He slowed once for a tractor, easing around the big green vehicle and giving a wave to the farmer—a man he'd known most of his life. Then he stepped on the gas once more. He did notice that the old farmer looked twice to see who was riding along with Chet. That would likely be the start of some hefty rumors. But then, being seen in town together would do more of the same. In a place the size of Hope, gossip fueled the community.

Hope was the kind of place that dropped like a splatter in the middle of Montana farmland. It had a couple of schools, a supermarket, a drugstore, an ice-cream parlor and a diner. The various shops catered to the rural clientele, offering everything from saddles to engine parts. Someone had tried to start up some uppity coffee joint a few years back, and it had tanked within six months. Hope took a certain amount of pride in remaining unchanged.

Chet pulled into Hope Ranch and Feed, which was located at the side of the highway just before town. The red-painted sign was cracked and peeling, and there were a few pickups in the parking lot. This store might not look like much—its forty-year-old display window showing an arrangement of horse-grooming products—but it was a necessity to pretty much everyone within fifty miles, and curb appeal wasn't needed to bring in the customers. A wide array of cattle ear tags, animal medicine, work wear and feed was draw enough for local ranchers. Anything a ranch might need could be bought right here—and if it couldn't be purchased off a shelf, it could be ordered.

"This is it," Chet said as he put the truck into Park.

Mack didn't move, and he caught the furrow in her brow as she looked out the window. Sometimes he forgot that she was new to this. Ten years had elapsed since her summers spent in Hope, and while he'd grown up on the land, she hadn't.

"You okay?" he asked, softening his voice.

"Fine."

"You're not getting out," he observed, a smile pulling at one side of his mouth. He had to hurry if he wanted to make his appointment at the credit union on time, and that was something he didn't want her to know about. When that finger of desperation wriggled up in his stomach, he didn't like an audience—especially not Mackenzie. It didn't fit in with the way he wanted her to see him.

She swung her gaze toward him and sighed heavily. "Will I ever actually belong here?"

It was a prudent question. The newest rancher around these parts had bought the land fifteen years ago, and he was still called "the new guy" and people continued to joke around about his not knowing his boot from his backside. Chet didn't want to lie to her, and he certainly wanted her to stick it out. How could he explain this?

"Depends on what you mean by *belong*," he said after a moment of thought. "It's like in a family—you get a role and you keep it. Around here, you'll probably always be the new one—that is, until someone else buys land and takes over that status. If you take over the newbie status, you'll be doing Chris Hoffman a favor. He came about fifteen years ago."

Mackenzie smiled faintly and shook her head. "That doesn't sound promising."

It didn't, and he knew that, but there was more to it. She might be the new one around town, but she'd be something different to him—something he wasn't willing to say aloud.

"Just don't let it bother you." That advice didn't cover any of the things he wanted to say, and he heard the empty-sounding promise they encompassed. He glanced at his watch. He'd be late if he wasn't careful. And he didn't know how to articulate this yet. He'd have to think on it, maybe sleep on it. The words would come eventually.

Why was it when he had the most to say, he had the fewest words?

"Now get out of my truck, and go shopping." He tossed her a grin, hoping to show her that there were no hard feelings.

"You're not coming?"

"I've got an errand to run," he said. "I'll call you when I'm done and I'll pick you up."

Mackenzie met his gaze, but her expression was undecipherable. She was feeling something, but she wouldn't let him see it.

"All right," she said. "I'll see you in a while."

She pushed open the door and jumped down, then slammed it shut behind her and headed toward the front door of Ranch and Feed. She didn't look back, and he realized that she'd fit

in better around here than she was giving herself credit for. The new one or not, she'd make
a place for herself. She was determined and
she looked good in a pair of cowboy boots.
He smiled at this thought, then put the truck
in Reverse.

Here's hoping that Andy didn't follow
through with his threat to sell all that pasture
to the highest bidder, or else he wouldn't be
around to see it.

If Chet thought that fitting into this town
was like fitting into a family, Mackenzie
would have more trouble than she'd anticipated. The Granger family appeared happy
and attractive. Chet and his brother were tall
and good-looking, Andy's six-foot-one frame
dwarfed by Chet's six-foot-five. Their father
had been the grizzled rancher, but even he'd
managed to make a pair of boots look better
for his feet being in them. All but a couple of
Chet's aunts were slim and their smiles were
always spontaneous and bright. From the outside, the Grangers were picture-perfect, and
they stood strong and united. This all sounded
good—so good that it might seem like a family
a woman would enjoy being a part of—but it
wasn't great if you were an outsider looking in.

The Grangers were loyal to each other, and in her experience, there wasn't a lot of room for anyone else in that family circle. They looked after family first. If Hope was like the Granger clan, she'd be out in the cold.

As Mackenzie stepped inside the store, she nodded to a man stacking up sacks of fertilizer on a pallet. He looked to be in his mid-sixties, his hair a tufted salt-and-pepper gray. He moved aside as she went by, and she could feel his eyes following her in idle interest. The store was lit by fluorescent lights, and an old-fashioned country tune jangled in the background.

"Are you Helen's granddaughter?" he asked.

Mackenzie turned back. "Yes. Mackenzie Vaughn."

"Harold Wright. Nice to meet you." He held out a callused hand and they shook. "I'm sorry about your grandmother. She'll be missed."

"Thanks." She pressed her lips together in acknowledgment. "Did you know her well?"

"Who didn't?" Harold cleared his throat. "She was a mainstay around here."

Another man came into the store, and Harold was diverted. She took the chance to turn down the first aisle, which sported plastic bags of ear tags, some bottles and nipples for calves, and a few different devices she didn't readily recognize.

The bell above the door jingled, and she noticed two women come inside. When they glanced at her, she put her attention into the next aisle, which held different-sized flat-backed buckets that could hang against a fence.

I should have paid more attention when I visited Granny, she mentally chastised herself. Frankly, she was a little too impressed with a supply store to feel confident in her abilities back at the ranch. At least she knew where to come when she needed anything. Chet had been right about this place, and perhaps it was better that she explore it alone. She'd need to be self-sufficient, since she was certain Chet wouldn't always be this available for her needs. He had his own ranch to run, and she wasn't about to take advantage of his kindness, either. His babysitting would come to an end.

One of the women came down the aisle where Mackenzie was browsing. She was in her forties with a short curly hairstyle that had a few strands of silver. She grabbed a couple of buckets and smiled at Mack.

"Hi there."

"Hi."

They moved past each other without any

further conversation, but Mackenzie had the distinct impression she was being sized up, not that she blamed anyone. Obviously, she was the new one, as Chet had pointed out, and she'd be a curiosity. The two women met up in the next aisle, and Mackenzie left them there, moving on to the aisle past them.

"Did you know that Andy Granger's back?" the first woman said to her companion, their voices filtering over to where Mack stood.

"Is he? For good?"

"No, apparently, he's just cooling his heels after a tiff with his fiancée. That wedding is off."

"Ah." The woman laughed knowingly. "That's Andy for you."

"So if you wanted another chance at him…" her friend teased. They laughed and the other woman's response mustn't have been verbal, because the topic seemed to die away. Clearly, these women didn't know that she was associated with the Granger family; otherwise, they wouldn't have been so comfortable gossiping within earshot, and she felt a niggle of anger at their casual discussion of Andy's life. He certainly wouldn't have been the first person to have relationship difficulties, but it sounded as if he'd dated one of the women. There was a lot she didn't know about him.

Mackenzie surveyed the shelves of large bottles. There was antiseptic, iodine, peroxide…except the bottles were the size of milk jugs, and a deworming medication suggested these were meant for animals, not people.

The women's conversation turned to Ida for a little while, and they sounded equally unsympathetic about Ida's situation as they did about Andy's. Of course, Mack had never met Ida, but Chet had a good opinion of her, and that made Mack inclined to like her…a far sight more than she liked these two women at the moment.

"So who says they're splitting up?" the first woman asked. "You can't always take that as gospel truth."

"Georgina's cousin." This seemed to be enough for the other woman but meant absolutely nothing to Mackenzie. How on earth had gossip spread this quickly?

"I feel a little bad for him," one said.

"Don't. Did you know that he's trying to get other families to sell their land to that developer?"

"The moron with the neon cowboy boots?" the other clarified.

"That's the one. Well, I've heard that if he can get other families to sell, too, they'll give him a cut. So if a little unhappiness comes his way, it's karma, if you ask me."

Mackenzie raised an eyebrow at that. Andy wasn't just thinking of selling... He was actively helping the developers find sales? She moved out of the aisle and stopped to look at an arrangement of salt blocks at the end.

She went to the front of the store to grab a handcart, and when she came back, the women were moving on to the next aisle, their arms full of merchandise already.

"I don't think that's true," Mackenzie said, and both women froze, looking at her in surprise.

"Sorry, sweetie?" the one with the short hair crooned.

"You're talking about Andy Granger," Mackenzie said. "And what you said isn't true."

"I have my sources," she replied and turned her back, and for a moment Mackenzie considered letting it go, but she was irritated already. She had started working with Chet, who'd never thought she was country enough, had inherited a ranch she didn't know how to run and had just been informed that Hope would accept her as easily as a family would—loaded words coming from a Granger—and she had no more patience.

"I know Andy," she said curtly. "He might have his faults, but he's a good guy."

"Crummy boyfriend, though," the other woman quipped.

"How is that your business?" Mackenzie retorted.

If these women had heard the deep sadness and longing in his voice when he talked to his ex-fiancée on the phone, they wouldn't have been able to judge him so harshly. Andy might have been irresponsible and disinterested in a ranching life, but that didn't make him the devil, either.

"And if you think that Andy is colluding with some big developer, you're nuts. He was born and raised here. Give him some credit for having a soul."

"Okay… Sorry." The women both squirmed in discomfort. "We didn't realize…"

She didn't have to finish the sentence, and they sidled away to the front counter to pay. Mackenzie had no desire to go stand behind them, so she stomped down another aisle until they'd paid up and left. Then she approached the counter with her purchase.

"You're an awful lot like Helen," Harold

said, a small smile twitching at one side of his mouth while he jabbed at the aged cash register with one finger.

"Sorry about that." She smiled at him. "I know Andy, is all."

"Me, too," Harold replied, and by his tone, she wasn't sure if that was a good thing or not. "But you stand by your friends, and your granny would be proud of that."

Her friends. Yes, the Grangers, for all their complicated history, were her friends, and she felt a certain amount of responsibility for Andy's reputation. Would they do the same for her? That was hard to tell, but at the very least, she'd be able to live with herself, and that was what mattered most.

After paying for her purchases, Mackenzie looked at her watch. It felt strange to be here in Hope without Granny around. It was lonelier, emptier. If Granny were here, she'd probably walk through the fabric shop with her, looking for material to make a quilt. But Granny wasn't here, and Mack didn't quilt. She had time to kill, and seeing as she was in town, she might as well make the most of it. Beauty's Ice Cream popped into her mind and she knew exactly what she needed right now—a double-scoop chocolate cone. It wouldn't solve anything, but it would be comforting all the same.

Chet heaved a sigh and pushed open the bank door, stepping back outside into the sunlight. The meeting hadn't gone well. The Grangers were well respected around these parts, but even they couldn't convince the bank to lend them twice what the land was worth.

He had a feeling that his brother was serious about selling, too, and Chet's options were shrinking. Irritation ate at him, and he stalked off toward his truck but paused when he saw Mackenzie ambling down the sidewalk toward him, a half-eaten ice-cream cone in one hand and a plastic bag in the other.

Great. Now he'd have that audience he hated so much, and he couldn't blame anyone for it but himself.

"Hi," Mackenzie said as she walked up. "I thought this was your truck."

"Yeah. Ready to go?"

He voice came out gruffer than he wanted it to, but he couldn't help it. He'd been hoping for more from this meeting—maybe a solution of some sort that he hadn't thought of yet—but these developers had more power than the townsfolk combined. They came with money, and people around here weren't wealthy.

Chet opened the door for her and gave her a hand up. Then he went around to the driver's side, his mind still whirring.

"I overheard a rumor or two in there," she said after they were both buckled up. She took another bite of ice cream as he put the truck into gear.

"Yeah? What kind of rumor?"

"That Andy is working with the developers to get people around here to sell."

"What?" Anger rose up inside him. "Andy wouldn't do that. Sell his own land? Maybe. But he'd never work with them. Who said this?"

"That's what I told them, and I don't know who they are. Two women in the store."

"Huh." Chet let out a grunt. Gossip was a given in a place this size, but it was still aggravating. "Anything else I should know about?"

"Oh, just talking about Andy and Ida being over." She shrugged. "Nothing to worry about."

At least that part was true, and as much as he wanted to fix things between his brother and Ida, he knew that he couldn't. A couple had to make it or break it on their own. Still, a small part of him wondered if Andy hadn't come back to see if Chet could help in that regard. Andy would never admit to that, though, even if it were true.

They pulled out onto the highway again. It ran alongside a railway track, and a train paced them, the rusted freight cars stretching out ahead of them in a straight line.

"Are you okay?" she asked after a moment.

"Yeah, fine. Why?"

"You don't seem fine." Her voice was gentle, and when he glanced over, he saw her looking at him, those blue eyes filled with concern. It had been a long time since a woman had cared about his feelings, and he found himself softening in spite of himself.

"I got turned down for a loan," he said after a moment. "At least, one big enough to match the developers."

"Oh, Chet…" Mackenzie slid a soft hand over his forearm. "I'm sorry."

"Yeah."

He didn't know what else to say. That was the crux of it all—he needed money to buy his brother out, and the bank wouldn't comply. He was being backed into a corner and he stood to lose the land he loved.

"You'll figure something out," she said after a moment of silence.

"Sure hope so," he replied. "You know, this land was always a source of conflict. My dad used to tell me the stories about it. I never thought it would do this to me and Andy, though."

"Yeah, tell me about it." She shot him a wan smile. "I inherited the land my father was supposed to get. He used to talk about what he'd do with the money when he finally sold the ranch, and then my grandmother died and left it to me. So I get it. When it comes down to an inheritance, things get dicey."

"What about the rest of the family?" Chet asked. "Are they mad, too?"

"Not thrilled. I have cousins, aunts and uncles. A lot of people were cut out for me to get this chance."

She understood better than he'd thought, and somehow that was comforting. This land could inspire the strongest of emotions in people—from love and devotion to jealousy and resentment. Someone always lost in the inheritance gamble. Someone always walked away with less than they'd hoped; with Mack's family, maybe nothing at all. But he could tell that her grandmother's ranch was more than just property for her.

"At least you got the whole ranch," he said.

"At what cost, though?" she murmured. "My dad and I haven't been close...not since the affair and all that. And now it's worse. Granny was pretty mad at Dad for what he did to Mom and me, and I think he can feel her disapproval from the grave. I can understand why your father gave you both half the land. He was probably trying to preserve something for you."

"I do know why he did it," Chet agreed quietly. "My dad always wanted Andy and me to be closer than we were. But we were so different. Even Dad had trouble really understanding Andy too well. It was a mess long before he ever died."

"And things with my dad were a mess long before Granny died," Mackenzie said. She was silent for a moment, and he thought that she'd finished with the topic when she added, her tone low, "At least Granny thought I was good enough for this land."

"Of course you're good enough." Chet cast her a puzzled glance. She'd already proven that she was up for the challenge. She'd thrown herself into the work and never complained once—more than Chet had expected. Obviously, Helen had known her granddaughter could handle it.

"You say that now," she replied, and there

was something sharp in her voice despite her soft tone.

"What are you talking about?"

"Look, Andy told me that when he and I were dating, you were against us from the first."

Chet looked over at her, confused. Against her? He'd been for her. He'd done his best to convince Andy that Mack was worth it—much as he was doing now with Ida. "He told you that?"

"He told me that you were the one who talked him into breaking up with me."

"It wasn't exactly like that," he said. In fact, it was downright wrong. Chet had sat his brother down and told him point-blank to choose between Mack and the other girl. He'd given him a guilt trip about fidelity and being honorable. It wasn't his fault that Andy had chosen the wrong girl.

"Then what was it like?"

They were nearing the side road that led to their ranches, and he slowed for the turn, his gaze locked on the road while his mind spun. A grassy trench lined each side of the highway, and the small green sign announced the side road with an innocuous number. Familiar fields stretched out beyond them—one side the Grangers' land and the other side hers.

He couldn't tell her what had really happened. Helen had made him promise to keep his mouth shut, and she'd had good reason for that. Mack already had issues enough with her father without adding a cheating ex-boyfriend into the mix.

Once they were on the gravel road, the sweet scent of fields flowing in the open windows, he said, "You were too good for him."

"So you broke us up because you thought I was so superior?" she asked incredulously. "And Ida's just mediocre enough to keep around?"

"Broke you up?" he retorted. "I told you it wasn't like that."

"Andy said if it weren't for you, he'd have seen a future between us," she said. "He was very clear about that. So while you say you didn't, I'm pretty sure you factored in."

He hadn't broken them up, but how was he supposed to prove that? His brother had lied to her, apparently, and she was blaming him for all of it. He hadn't seen this one coming.

"You're better off without him," Chet said. "Just leave it at that."

Mackenzie pulled a hand through her hair, tugging the blond tendrils away from her face. She looked as if she was about to speak a couple of times but stopped. Finally, she said, "So tell me this—why is Ida better Granger material than I was?"

Chet shook his head. Better for Andy? It wasn't about that. It was about Andy being a moron, but he couldn't explain all of this. It was over and done with. It was ten years behind them. She was better off just letting it all go.

There was a very big difference between his feelings for Ida and his feelings for Mack. Ida had his respect and he'd been looking forward to having her as part of the family. She'd have been good for Andy, good for the Grangers and a great addition to Thanksgiving dinner. But he'd never imagined something more with Ida. He'd never fallen in love with her. With Mack, he'd imagined much more, longed for a chance to hold her close… And when he'd told his brother to choose Mackenzie, he'd been doing the right thing in spite of his feelings for her.

"I told you," he said slowly and clearly. "I wasn't against you."

And that was all he could say.

Chapter 6

When Chet pulled up to her house, Mackenzie gathered the handles of the plastic bags holding the salt licks in one hand. A graceful exit would be best—not that she was even sure she could pull one off. The last couple of minutes of their ride together had been in silence, the big cowboy next to her seeming to almost vibrate with tension. She was confident that he'd rather be anywhere but in this truck with her. Whatever he was feeling, he wasn't saying aloud, and the closer they got to home, the more Mack wished she could just put this whole trip behind her.

Chet turned into her drive and eased to a stop in front of the low ranch house.

"Thanks for the ride." She wouldn't be surprised if it was the last he ever offered.

Mackenzie pushed open the door and slid down from the passenger seat. Chet cleared his throat, drawing her gaze back over her shoulder. Those gray eyes were pinned on her again, and she could see conflicted emotion swimming there.

"Look—" he scrubbed a hand through his hair "—I don't know what you heard, but I never thought you were beneath Andy."

She wasn't sure what he wanted from her, and she paused, one hand on the open truck door, the other full with the bags. What good did rehashing this even do? It didn't change what had happened.

"Maybe you were just looking out for your brother. We can leave it at that."

Did she really want to hear the truth about why she hadn't measured up when Ida had? She knew her own flaws, but hearing them repeated by Chet wouldn't exactly make her feel any better. Maybe it was just better to agree— Ida, whoever she was, was a better choice.

"I *was* looking out for him—" He bit off the

words and shook his head. "It was more complicated than that, though."

"Did I get between you and Andy or something?" she asked.

"No. Of course not. Andy and I had issues that predated you, trust me. He was lucky to have you. I always knew that." He thumped his hands on top of the steering wheel, his frustration obvious.

She blinked. Lucky? He had a funny way of showing it. But since they were already discussing this, she might as well get the answers she'd been wanting for the past ten years.

"So why convince him to dump me, then?" she asked.

"I can't go into exactly what happened," he said. "Suffice it to say, I didn't convince him to dump you."

"You—" She stopped, her mind going over all the information she had about that breakup. "Andy said that it was because you convinced him—"

"If I did, that wasn't my intention," he interrupted. "I never told him not to be with you. I wasn't trying to break you up."

"So what did you say to him?" she pressed.

He was silent for a long moment, then

sighed. "Some things should stay between brothers. I owe him that much."

And there it was—that door closing again between the Granger family and everyone else. Of course he'd side with his brother—he always did! So how come Ida got to stick her foot in the door?

"Okay, well…fine." She adjusted the bags in her hand—they were starting to feel heavy. "Thanks again for the ride."

She slammed the door and turned toward the house. It shouldn't have mattered as much as it seemed to. She had no desire to be with Andy—this was about Chet. She knew that much. She cared what Chet thought of her, felt about her… She hated that Ida had gained his trust and his good opinion, while she hadn't. From what she could tell, Ida wasn't a country girl, either, so what did she have that Mackenzie didn't?

A warm wind rustled through two big elms in the front yard, and the scent of warm grass and lilacs met her with a comforting embrace. The Grangers had never been anything but complicated, but her grandmother had always managed to make her feel safe and secure, and the smell of the summer breeze brought her grandmother's memory back so strongly that she felt tears prick her eyes.

Mack glanced back once and found Chet's gaze trained on her, his expression like granite. He raised two fingers in a salute, then turned his attention to the mirrors and the truck crunched backward. She headed straight to the front door, and when she got there, she looked back again to see the truck pulling out onto the road.

What had he meant about not being the one to convince Andy to dump her? That had been Andy's story—there was no room for miscommunication there. So which one of them was lying? And if Chet hadn't done it, why would he protect Andy's lie? But the Granger brothers were like that—they had each other's backs. It seemed she had their backs, too, because when Andy was being trashed by those women in Ranch and Feed, she'd done what felt right and stood up for him. The Grangers were protected on all sides. But who had her back when she needed it?

Mack opened the front door and dropped her bags on the wooden floorboards. Her cell phone started to ring at that moment, and she dug it out of her pocket on the fourth ring. It was her father's number, and she closed her eyes as she picked up the call.

"Hello?"

"Hi, Mackie, how are things at Granny's?"

He refused to call the ranch hers, and the old annoyance spiked inside her. "I'm good. How are you, Dad?"

She tossed her keys onto a narrow hall table covered in a white doily that hung down the sides. It would be hard to empty out all of these little corners that had Granny's touch to them, and she wasn't sure that she ever would. She felt as if they kept her here, somehow—kept her memory more vibrant.

"Good...good..." He cleared his throat. "How is your mother?"

"She asked me not to tell you anything about her." Her parents hadn't even bothered keeping a good ex-relationship going. As her mother had put it, Mackenzie was grown, so what was the point?

"So that hasn't changed, huh?" Her father sounded irritated. "It's been a decade, for crying out loud. How long is she going to hold a grudge?"

"No idea, Dad." She still had a pretty hefty grudge going, too, if that counted for anything. "But let's not talk about Mom." It felt like betrayal to discuss her behind her back, anyway.

"Then let's talk about you," he said. "I've

stumbled across something I think you're really going to like."

"Oh?" She was only half listening as she ambled toward the kitchen. She needed to grab a quick snack before heading out to check on the animals, and her mind was moving ahead to her chores.

"A horse stable."

"What?" She paused in the act of opening the fridge.

"A horse stable." He repeated it matter-of-factly. "There's one for sale just outside Billings. Business is booming. You wouldn't believe how many city folk want to own their own horses for riding but obviously don't have the space to keep them. So this stable houses and cares for the horses—all for various fees, of course—and it's doing very, very well."

"And what does this have to do with me?" she asked, pulling a loaf of bread and some bologna out of the fridge.

"It's for sale. For less than what you'd get for the ranch."

So he wanted her to sell? She knew her father had been deeply hurt when he was cut from Granny's will, but was he actually out looking for places she could buy instead?

"Dad, this is Granny's ranch. It isn't just

some plot of land somewhere—it's…" Did she really have to explain this to her own father?

"It's old. It's run-down. It's a whole lot of work to run if you try to stick it out. I don't know if Granny ever told you, but the neighbors, the Grangers, have been interested in buying Granny out for years. If you wanted to sell—"

"You think they'd be interested," she concluded.

"I know they'd be interested," he replied. "About a month before Granny died, she mentioned it to me again—that Granger offered to buy her out. He wants to expand, and he wants it bad."

"Chet?" she asked.

"That's him."

She'd suspected that Chet's interest in the land was more than simple neighborly goodwill, but the past few days together had worked to reassure her. Chet didn't seem as though he wanted to take over—he seemed as though he actually wanted her to stick around. In fact, he hadn't offered to buy her out once. Her father's casual comments sparked that old suspicion. Men could lie, especially if they had enough motive to do so. Chet had just been turned down for a loan at the bank, and he'd seemed pretty deflated by it all. She doubted that he had any more cards up his sleeve. If Andy sold the pasture, buying her out would be the next logical step…if she were willing to sell, that was. Could all of his friendship, his offer of help—could it all have been aimed at softening her up for the ultimate request to buy her out?

"Look, Mackie." Her father's tone softened. "Running a ranch is a huge amount of work. If you buy an already thriving business, then it's a whole lot less grunt work for you to do. That means time to travel, too, might I add. It just makes financial sense. That ranch isn't worth much more than the land that you're sitting on right now, but a business like this one would keep the money flowing into your pocket, where it belongs."

"Granny wanted me to try this—"

"Granny was a bitter old woman," her father snapped. Then he sighed. "I don't mean to discount the memories and all that, but if I'm not sentimentally attached to that old ranch, then why should you feel any obligation? I was just thinking practically. Just looking out for my daughter. If Granger wants to buy it, I'd suggest you sell."

Mackenzie suspected that her father would be relieved to have the ranch sold and forgotten—a painful memory eliminated. Her first instinct when her father suggested anything was to say no, but there was something about his prospect that did intrigue her—it was the best of both worlds. She could have horses in her life but still have the city, too. She missed her friends, nice restaurants and coffee shops that required more than a size when ordering.

Half-caf, extra whip, double shot of hazelnut had been her order, and she missed that perfect first sip. The city hadn't been misery. She'd had good times there, too.

Sunday morning brunch had always been nice, and right about now she'd be willing to kill for a perfectly poached eggs Benedict. Then there had been the bookstores afterward, where she'd wander through and pick up some cards or a new novel to read...

Hope was a cute little town, but she'd never be one of them, not truly, while Billings was the city she'd grown up in. It did make sense. Plus, there were buyers right now—something she couldn't always take for granted.

"I'll think about it," she said.

"This could be really good for you, you know. When I heard about the stable, you were all I could think of."

"So how did you hear about it?" she interrupted.

"Krissy's aunt is the one selling it."

Of course. Those generous feelings for her father evaporated. Krissy was her father's latest girlfriend. The woman who'd broken up her parents' marriage hadn't lasted the first year, but Krissy had seemed to hang on. She was only about ten years older than Mackenzie, and Mack had seen pictures of her posted on her father's Facebook page with them sitting all relaxed on her father's deck, Krissy's pedicured feet in his lap. There were countless photos of them doing things together—hiking, eating brunch, cooking… Mackenzie had to admit that she resented their implied happiness. He should have tried harder to have that with her mother. If he'd put a little more effort into the family he had—maybe taken a few idealized photos of them once in a while— things might have turned out a lot differently. The fact that the stable was linked to Krissy's family made the prospect a little less appealing, but once she owned it herself, Krissy's family would be out of the picture. And who knew how long Krissy would last, anyway? With any luck, Krissy would get tired of dating someone old enough to be her father and take off with someone her own age. Spiteful as it was, Mackenzie thought her father could benefit from a little heartbreak. At least he could see how it felt to be dumped.

"Uh, speaking of Krissy..." her father went on, his voice going up a little. He was tense or excited. She knew the sound in his voice—the sound he got when he bought a new car. "I have some news."

"Oh?" She tried to keep her tone uninterested, but her Spidey sense was tingling.

"We're getting married." His voice glowed warm with satisfaction, and she sat in silence, processing the information. Seriously? Krissy was willing to marry him? Had he proposed? Had he done something embarrassing like get down on one knee in the middle of a restaurant, or put her ring in the bottom of a champagne flute?

"Mackenzie?"

"I'm here," she said weakly. "When?"

"We haven't set a date yet, but Krissy doesn't want to put it off too long."

"Well, congratulations." She didn't feel even remotely happy for him.

"We want you to be there, of course," he went on. "It wouldn't be the same without you. Krissy was thinking maybe a destination wedding, and I'd be happy to foot the bill—"

"I don't need you to pay my way," she said tersely.

"You're my little girl," her father said. "I just wanted to do this for you, like a gift."

"I'm running a ranch now," she said, and she didn't mean to sound as cold as she did, rubbing in the inheritance all over again, but she was still processing this news of his engagement. "I can't just take off on a vacation. I have cattle, goats, land... I can't promise anything right now."

"I'm sure you can get someone to take over." He sounded mildly incredulous. He'd grown up here after all, so he couldn't be oblivious to the running of it. "I know this is probably a bit of a surprise, but—"

"Dad, I have to go." She sucked in a deep breath. "Congratulations to you and Krissy."

"Okay, okay..." He sighed. "What should I tell her aunt about the stable?"

"Tell her I'll think about it," she said. "But I've got to go."

"Take care, Mackie. I love you."

She mumbled an "I love you" in return, then gratefully hung up the phone. Her first thoughts were for her mother, who hadn't remarried. It hardly seemed fair that the one who'd done the cheating moved on first, but ten years wasn't exactly a rebound, either. She should be happy for his happiness. That was the mature thing, wasn't it? She shouldn't hold his mistake against him forever. She knew these things, but it wasn't so easy when it came to her emotions.

Would she go to his wedding? Not if she could get out of it. While her father seemed eager to rebuild a relationship with her recently, she couldn't forget about the years when she hadn't seemed to matter to him at all. He'd been working late—presumably with some girl-friend—and he'd missed a lot of her adolescence. Her mother had been the one to comfort her after her first breakup, to talk her through dating jitters, to help her fill out college applications and to listen to her teenage woes. Her mother had been there; her father had been off gallivanting, pretending that his wife and daughter didn't exist. Back then, they'd thought he was working and they'd tried to be understanding. Now they knew differently, and she was having a hard time forgiving that. She had no intention of being duped again.

So now her father's life was shiny and new again, with a fiancée, an upcoming wedding and Facebook pictures of blissful couplehood. And she had no desire to stand smiling in the photos.

* * *

That evening, Chet sat at the kitchen table, a mug of coffee between his palms. His left shoulder ached from a wrench he'd received when a bull got testy with him earlier. He'd caught himself against the fence, but there had been something just off about the angle, because he'd felt the burn in his shoulder before the pain hit. That would take a bit of healing. He reached up and massaged the area, grimacing slightly against the pain.

This was the job around here—it required a hard body and a sharp mind. If either started to slip, you'd better hope it was the body that went first, in his humble opinion. When you were being sized up by a one-ton bull, your brawn wasn't much of a match. Unfortunately, when this particular ton of beef had been sizing him up, his mind had been still half on Mackenzie.

He'd gone over the conversation with her in his mind all afternoon, and the more he thought about it, the more frustrated he felt. He wanted to tell her the truth—that Andy had cheated on her and that he'd told his idiot little brother to do the right thing. But if he told her that, he'd be breaking a promise to her late grandmother, and Chet was a man who stood by his word.

The promise she'd evoked from him had been no casual agreement. She'd been certain that if Mack knew the truth, it would set her up for trust issues for the rest of her life, and maybe the old lady had been right. Mack had felt abandoned by her father when he left the family for another woman, and if her first love had cheated on her, too, he could see how that could mess with someone's mind. He was no expert on women, but he could sympathize, at least. But how long was he supposed to sit on this?

Sometimes it took a bigger man to hold a secret than to unload it on someone else. Helen Vaughn had asked him to keep a secret, and she was not someone to ask this sort of favor lightly. She was a wiry little woman who believed in honesty, family, church and an American's right to bear arms. In that order. She wouldn't have asked this unless she knew it was necessary.

Things were complicated now. Chet rolled his shoulder slowly, testing the limits of his movements. It was a strain, nothing more. He'd done worse damage to himself in the past. What he needed to do was to get Andy back home to Ida. That could take care of a small part of the problem, at least, and he could start unknotting the rest of it with a little elbow room.

The back door opened and Andy sauntered in. He blew out a sigh and tossed his hat onto the counter. He looked tired but not dirty. Chet was willing to bet that his brother hadn't spent much time riding with other ranch hands today, by the look of him.

"What's for supper?" Andy asked.

"I already ate," Chet replied. "Leftovers are in the fridge, if you're interested."

Andy made a face and pulled open the fridge.

"So where were you?" Chet asked.

"I headed over to Rickton to check out some new rims for my truck," he replied, emerging from the fridge with a plastic-wrapped plate of chicken fingers and a bowl of mashed potatoes.

"Ah."

Andy sent him a quizzical look. "What's wrong with that?"

"There are a few rumors going around town about you." So much for easing into it, but his shoulder ached, and he didn't have the patience to dance around this.

"Always are," Andy shot back with a grin. "What are they this time?"

"That you're colluding with that developer to get other families to sell," Chet said, keeping his eyes locked on his brother, waiting for a response. He wanted to see shock, an eye roll—something to prove his brother's innocence—but Andy froze.

"Tell me that's just some overactive imagination," Chet said quietly.

"They asked me to see if anyone else wanted to sell," Andy said, his voice low. "I may have mentioned it to Watson. But that doesn't mean I'm colluding with anyone. It's a good deal. I'm planning on taking it myself. I think you should, too—"

"And does Watson want to sell?" Chet asked tightly.

"Not a chance." Andy shook his head. "I don't really care about old Watson. I wanted to convince you. Thing is, we might be able to drive the price up a bit. Four hundred acres… We could make a fortune, Chet."

"I told you before that I won't sell."

"What if you could make enough to buy a ranch twice the size of this one, free and clear?" Andy asked, raising an eyebrow. "If you want to ranch, you can ranch, brother. But you could do it comfortably, with the newest equipment and a nice reliable staff. Who says you have to bare-bones it like you do now?"

There was some logic to what his brother was saying. Chet certainly wasn't getting rich this way, but Andy's proposition wasn't taking into account that this land had been in the Granger family for generations. Their great-grandparents had even been buried on this land. You didn't just walk away from something like that.

"And what's in it for you?" Chet asked. "I mean, Watson selling. Or me, for that matter."

Andy looked away. "They mentioned giving me a percentage of the other sales if I could interest them."

"A kickback. How much?"

"Five percent."

Chet stared at his brother, stunned. "Five percent? And you don't feel the least bit bad about any of this?"

"I didn't say that I accepted," Andy retorted. "I said that they offered."

"Fine." Chet sighed.

"Look, Chet. When I say that we'd be rich, I mean that we'd be seriously loaded. If they want to offer a kickback, we could take it—split it. I'm not suggesting that we convince everyone else to sell. I'm thinking about you and me."

"It's not all about money," Chet said. "You know that. Or you should."

"Just think about it," Andy said.

It looked as though the Hope rumor mill

had been more accurate than he'd cared to admit, and the realization hit Chet like a blow to the gut. Had his brother really moved that far away from the values they were brought up with? Their parents had raised them with church once a week and family for the rest of the time. Family had meant everything to the Grangers, and when their mother died of cancer, their aunts had stepped in to be maternal figures for them—a job those women took seriously. He and Andy had grown up in a tangle of cousins on this very land. It was one thing for Andy to make his life in the city, but it was another to sell out their childhood home—their entire community—to some faceless developer.

"Andy, please don't do this." He hated the pleading that he heard in his voice, but he had no choice. His brother could end his ranching career here on the family land with one signature on a dotted line. The thought made his stomach churn.

Andy didn't say anything, and Chet sighed. He wouldn't beg again.

"Have you talked to Ida?" Chet asked after a moment.

"Not really your business, man," Andy replied.

Maybe it wasn't his business, but it wasn't

as if Chet had wanted to be in the middle of his brother's relationship issues. Andy had landed on his doorstep and effectively muddied those waters. Besides, Ida had been more than good for him, she'd been a calming influence. When Andy got worked up about some idea, she was the one who could talk him back down. If Andy got back together with Ida, it might just be the cure that Chet needed, too. Was that terrible of him to hope for?

In spite of everything happening with Andy right now, he did want his brother to be happy, and he didn't look that way at the moment. The last time Chet had seen him happy had been before their father passed away. Just after he'd proposed to Ida.

"You aren't going to talk to her?" Chet asked.

"She kicked me out!" Andy's voice rose. "When a woman kicks you out—"

"You go back and figure out how to fix it!" Chet interrupted. Andy had always bailed too early. That was one lesson he hadn't learned on the ranch—holding on.

"Yeah, and this is based on how much personal experience?" his brother countered. "You've never been engaged. You hardly even date. I fail to see how you're qualified to give any kind of advice on women!"

His words stung because they were true. While Andy had been out with girls, Chet had been learning the ins and outs of running a ranch. Someone had to learn it, and someone had to run this place. So far, Andy stood to reap a whole lot of money if he sold his part of the inheritance, and Chet stood to lose—none of which took into account the years of hard work he'd put into this place while his brother started up a life in the city.

"I'm pretty confident about the basics," Chet said coldly. "Like standing by your word."

"So I should marry her, even if we're wrong for each other?" Andy spat the words out with venom. "We're not married, Chet. We're not even engaged anymore. It didn't work out!"

"It's about principles," Chet snapped. "With Ida, with the developers…all of it!"

"Your high principles didn't get you far. You're single and lonely, and you put all your attention into my life instead of getting one of your own."

"I'm trying to save you from making the biggest mistake of your life!" Chet spat back.

"Are you?" Andy demanded. "It looks to me like you've got more invested in my engagement than I do."

"That's sad."

"It is," Andy agreed snidely. "Get a life of your own."

"I have one!"

He had a ranch that he loved more deeply than Andy would ever appreciate. He had a community that respected him, a family he cared about... Chet couldn't keep his anger in check anymore. This was how his brother saw him, as some pathetic wannabe, getting his satisfaction from other people's relationships? There could be nothing further from the truth! If he could walk away from any feelings of responsibility for his younger brother, he would, but Chet was made of sterner stuff than that.

Chet didn't hold himself back out of fear or weakness. He held himself back because he believed in right and wrong. Andy had no idea how much Chet had restrained himself. There had been many a time that Andy had hurt Mack's feelings and he'd seen that dangerous flash in her eyes, and Chet had never once taken advantage of their little tiffs. He'd never once told her how he felt about her—asked her to choose him instead. He'd have been good to Mack. He'd have been faithful—which was a far sight more than Andy had been.

"You'd be grateful to know how much I've

held myself back," Chet said, his voice dangerously low.

"A lot of good it's doing you," his brother scoffed. "Do me a favor and let loose for once. Maybe you'd leave my life alone. So back off!"

Chet slammed his hands on the table, and a glass wobbled, sloshing water.

"You're an idiot, Andy," he growled. "And I'm washing my hands of you."

He strode past his brother and banged open the back door. He couldn't be in that room with Andy for another minute without driving his fist right into his brother's smug face. A hot ball of rage rose up through his abdomen, and he wished he could hit something—anything to release this anger.

But he wouldn't.

Maybe Andy was right. Maybe he'd held himself back too much all these years. Maybe he should have forgotten about his duty to his brother, his duty to his family and all of those principles of his and done what he'd dreamed of doing every single day of that long, hot summer when Mack had been at the ranch next door. Maybe he should have told her how he felt, how he longed for her, how he dreamed of her…

As for Andy's broken engagement, Chet was

done. If Ida had seen the light, all the power to her. Maybe she could find a decent guy who'd treat her better than Andy seemed to do.

His boots thumped against the hard earth, and he sucked in a lungful of that cool evening air. The sun had already sunk below the horizon, a scarlet splash glowing across the sky. A few wispy clouds down by the horizon glowed gold, and the rage started to seep out of him.

There was something about the Montana sky that was big enough to absorb all those clashing emotions, and he turned his steps toward the barn.

He'd do one last check of the horses. If the sky wasn't sufficient, then the soft welcoming nicker from the stables was normally enough to work the knots out of his neck and shoulders. He slowed his steps, the anger pulsing like a distant drumbeat in his head. Andy obviously thought he was some loser, living vicariously through his brother, and he could probably handle that, but what he couldn't handle was his brother's declaration about Mackenzie. Just the thought of Andy trying his charms on Mack again set Chet's blood to boiling.

The barn loomed against the backdrop of the sunset, a black shape against a crimson sky. Except the barn door wasn't closed, and a sliver of light shone from within. Chet picked up his pace.

His first thought was that one of the ranch hands was doing some extra work—not a likely scenario. Or maybe one of his employees was trying to steal from him—a whole lot more likely. He paused at the door, nudged it open wider, then slipped inside, stepping as quietly as possible. The gentle nicker of one of the sleepy horses greeted him before all of his fears evaporated. There was no wayward ranch hand here. On the ground next to Butter Cream and the little white buckling crouched Mackenzie.

Chapter 7

While fighting with his brother, his mind had been firmly on Mack, on the things he hadn't done when he'd wanted to so badly, and here she was in front of him. But this wasn't the seventeen-year-old Mackenzie; this was the woman—mature, developed, intriguing. He'd restrained himself before for good reason— she'd been his brother's girl. But she wasn't any longer, and he was tired of holding himself behind that wall of reserve.

Chet stood motionless for a moment, watching Mackenzie murmur to the mama goat. Butter Cream was stoically ignoring her, and Mackenzie sighed, pulling her slender fingers through her long hair. She pushed herself up to a standing position, her back still to him.

"Mack..."

She whipped around, eyes wide with surprise, then laughed breathily. "Chet! You scared me."

"Butter Cream came for a visit?" he asked wryly, nodding to the goat.

"Afraid so. She left Chocolate Truffle and took her other baby for a walk. I've been calling her Extra Whip."

She certainly had her grandmother's knack for naming critters. He smiled faintly. "Why's that?"

"I miss my fancy coffee." Her eyes sparkled at her own little joke. "She got in around the back. I was just trying to lure her out this way."

Another oversight by a worker, but he wasn't in any mood to be dealing with his ranch hands tonight. He was tempted to ask her to show him where, but he was better than that. He wasn't going to make excuses to be with her. If she was here, he wanted it to be because she wanted to be.

"Chet, are you okay?"

No, he wasn't okay, and she seemed to be able to zero in on him when he was at his worst. He sighed and stepped all the way inside, pulling the door shut behind him. "It's been one of those nights."

"What happened?"

He couldn't tell her all of it—not the part about Andy taking a kickback on land sales. That was something so infuriating that he still needed to sit with it and chew it over. It wasn't something he could put into words yet, even though it ate away at his middle. He glanced up to find Mack looking at him, her blue eyes soft and sympathetic. She wanted to know what had happened. He could tell her about Ida, at least. That would be part of the burden shared.

"I butted my nose into my brother's business with Ida."

Chet nodded toward the opposite end of the barn, where there were some low bales of hay. They walked slowly in that direction, past the horses' stalls. Butter Cream followed them passively enough—him, really. He knew the goat would go wherever he went, and part of his reason for not wanting to simply take this goat was that Butter Cream brought Mackenzie over so often, too. He'd be crazy to cut off that avenue to the pretty novice rancher.

"So he was mad?" she clarified.

"Something like that."

His brother's words were still echoing in his

head, and they stung enough that he wasn't
about to repeat them. Not yet. Not until he could
say them aloud and roll his eyes, but the fact that
his brother thought so poorly of him rankled.

"Things were said," Chet said drily. "I came
out to get some air."

"So is he leaving, then?" she asked.

Chet laughed bitterly. "That would be too easy!
No, he's not leaving. He's just incensed that I'd
dare impose on his privacy. Ironically enough."

As if Andy weren't imposing on Chet's privacy by showing up on his doorstep.

"I thought of all people, he could talk to
you," she said.

"When we were kids, he'd talk to Mom.
When Mom died, he—" Chet frowned. Who
had Andy turned to after her death? To him. At
least sometimes. Chet had turned to their father for support, and Andy had turned to him.

"I remember you guys being closer—the
Granger boys."

"I guess we were." He'd hated it, truth be
told, but he didn't like talking about that side of
things. This wasn't the relationship he wanted
with his brother, but whenever they got into the
same room together lately, they ended up argu-
ing over something—anything. If he'd known
how to fix it, he would have.

Mackenzie sat down on a bale of hay, and Chet settled next to her. The straw prickled into his jeans, and he glanced down at her—that golden hair shining in the barn's low light.

"Andy and my dad never got along too well," Chet said after a moment. "Dad and I connected over the ranch, and Andy... I don't know. He didn't care about the stuff we did."

"You left him out."

Her succinct insight irked him. "He walked away," he countered.

Mack shrugged, and Chet looked at the floor. Sure, Chet felt guilty about monopolizing their father's time, but he'd been a kid, too. He hadn't known how to keep those balances, nor should it have been expected of him. And Andy had been a smart aleck who kept pushing the limits. They sat in silence for a few beats, her warm, slender arm brushing against his.

"Speaking of difficult relationships with fathers..." she said quietly. "My dad called. He told me that he's getting married."

"Oh yeah?" Chet eyed her cautiously. Was this good news or bad? He wasn't sure how it would land until she glanced up at him through her long lashes. Her expression was grim.

"Her name is Krissy, and she's only about

ten years older than me. They've been together for a while now."

"Have you met her before?" he asked.

"No." She rested against the pile of bales behind her. "I never wanted to. I hardly see my dad as it is, and I wasn't exactly keen to meet his latest girlfriend. They never last." She winced. "Except for this one, apparently."

Chet nodded. "So you're not exactly wishing them well?"

"No." She turned away, her hair falling over her profile so he couldn't see what she was feeling. He could guess, though. This wouldn't be easy on her—it wouldn't be easy on anyone—and he wished there was a way he could lighten the burden.

"I get it. It would just feel better somehow if he knew exactly how much he lost when he walked away from you two—a little karmic backlash."

"Exactly." Her smile warmed him. "Karmic backlash. I like that. They actually look happy—in the pictures, at least." She sighed and leaned back once more against the bales. "And it's not only that I don't want him to move on—it's that I don't think it's fair that my cheating father gets to find a really good match for him and the rest of us don't."

"Andy would say it's because he takes chances," Chet said.

"And tossed away a twenty-year marriage," she responded.

She had an excellent point. He'd wondered over the years how her father had been able to just walk away. Mack's mom was a timeless beauty, much like her daughter. Where had things gone wrong?

"Maybe he regrets his mistakes more than you think," Chet suggested. He couldn't imagine a man not regretting that. She cast him a sidelong look, and he smiled. She didn't want to hear that. "So you haven't forgiven him yet?"

"Not yet."

Her pale hand rested on the stubbly hay between them, and he slid his hand over hers. Her skin was warm and smooth, and instead of pulling away, she leaned over and put her head on his shoulder. The scent of her shampoo—or was it perfume?—mingled with the aroma of hay and horses. Everything was so quiet, and having her snuggled against him felt better than he'd imagined it would.

"Why can't men just be straightforward?" she asked.

"Some of us are."

She'd never seen him as a real option, but he was the kind of man who would have stood by her, loved her. His eye would never have wandered.

"Well, you, of course," she said—and her tone was so casual he was mildly stunned. "You're one of those old-fashioned types whose handshake is as good as a contract."

She sat up again, the spot on his shoulder where she'd rested suddenly feeling empty. So she knew that he was a good one? Even though there were so many things he couldn't tell her, he was glad that she'd picked up on that. But when they were teenagers, she'd never looked his way. Andy had won, fair and square.

"What's wrong with having some principles?" he asked.

"Nothing," she replied with an apologetic shrug. "Only that you're the last of them under sixty."

Her smile was teasing, but he heard the message underneath. She wanted an honest, reliable man, just not him. That smarted a little, but it also sparked a challenge. He'd never acted on his feelings, not wanting to offend, not wanting to overstep. A part of him wanted to change the way she saw him.

"Chet, can I ask you something?" She turned

to him, blue eyes looking almost navy in the light. Her cheeks were a light pink, and he had an urge to reach out and run the back of a finger down that silky cheek. He had to jerk his mind back from the precipice.

"Of course."

"Are you going to ask to buy my land?"

He blinked. Where had that come from? "I thought you wanted to run it."

She sighed. "There's a stable just outside Billings. Krissy's aunt is selling it, and my dad's suggestion was to unload the ranch and buy the stable."

She said it so casually that the words didn't hit him until a moment later. Sell? Was she considering it?

"Are you interested?" he asked, trying to keep his tone as casual as hers.

"I don't know. It isn't a bad idea. I mean, Granny's ranch needs a lot of work, and it's going to stay a lot of work. This stable, if managed properly, could almost run itself. According to my dad, at least."

He didn't say anything. It really wasn't his place to tell her what to do with her own land and her own money. When he'd heard that she was coming back, he hadn't let himself think about it too much. He'd been curious to see her—wanted her to see him in the best light, of course—but he'd kept any kind of hope firmly quashed. Then she'd arrived and they'd started spending time together, and he hadn't realized how much he'd been allowing himself to feel lately until this moment, when the thought of her leaving was like a lead weight in his stomach. If she wanted him to make this decision easier for her by offering to buy her out, he wouldn't do it.

"You haven't offered to buy me out," she said after a second.

"No, I haven't." His tone was more brusque than he'd intended. He looked over at her, and he found those blue eyes fixed on him in an expression of uncertainty. Her gaze flickered down.

"In your honest opinion, can I do this?"

"Run this place?"

"Yes." She looked up again, and she was so close that he could easily have slid an arm around her waist and pulled her against him.

"You bet. Like you said, it's hard work, but you could do this." He swallowed. "If it was what you wanted."

Having her this close was too much like those times when Mack had been dating Andy and Chet had been keeping his distance, at least emotionally. He could still remember the way she used to lean over the fence, her eyes squinted against the sun. She used to watch him work when Andy wasn't around, and it had taken all his effort to keep himself working, to keep himself from walking over there and pulling her solidly into his arms and forgetting about his principles.

Of course, he never had.

"Would I be able to do it without you, though?" she pressed. "I mean, without your help and advice?"

"You mean if Andy sells and I can't stay," he clarified, the words almost sticking in his throat.

"Worst-case scenario…"

"Everyone needs advice," he said quietly. "Doesn't need to be mine."

Everyone needed love, too, but she didn't have to get any of it from him. Even if he wanted to be that man in her life so badly that he could taste it. She dropped her gaze and rubbed a hand down her bare arm. The golden light from the overhead fixture made her hair glow, and he had an overwhelming desire to close that distance between them. He stopped.

"Mack—" His voice caught as he said her name, and she turned toward him again. This time, he didn't stop himself. He didn't rein it in, and he didn't ask permission. He brushed a tendril of honey-colored hair away from her cheek, then slid his hand behind her neck, burying his fingers in the silken warmth of her hair. He tugged her toward him, and she followed his movement, her eyes widening in momentary surprise and her lips parting slightly as if she was about to say something.

He paused, his mouth hovering over hers, waiting for her protest, and when it didn't come, he lowered his lips ever so lightly onto hers. She sucked in a breath as their lips met, and at first she was perfectly still. It started out gently, but when she moved into him, he deepened the kiss and slipped his other arm around her waist, pulling her against him, and if he weren't as soundly principled as he was, he wouldn't have stopped there.

He'd wondered what this would be like for a decade—how she'd feel in his arms, how he'd feel with his lips on hers—and right now all he could think was that he didn't want this moment to end.

Mackenzie pulled back, and he reluctantly released her. A hand fluttered up to her lips.

"Oh…" she breathed.

"I've been wanting to do that for a decade,"

he said huskily. He brushed a hair away from her face and shrugged apologetically.

She laughed shakily, and when her eyes met his, he was tempted—so very tempted—to do that all over again...

"I think I'd better get back," she said.

"Yeah, me, too."

His brain was pounding in time to the beat of his heart, and he couldn't entirely think straight. He'd had reasons for holding back until now—good ones. He needed to get his mind straight again before he did something he regretted.

Mackenzie stood up and straightened her shirt. She looked back at him briefly. Her cheeks were flushed and her eyes shone. Then she bent and patted Butter Cream's side, then scooped up the kid, and miraculously, the goat obediently followed her toward the door of the barn.

"Good night," he called, his low voice reverberating through the barn.

"Sleep tight, Chet—" Her voice was soft, and it was clipped off by the closing of the barn door, leaving him alone with the animals.

Sleep tight. He smiled to himself. *Not a chance tonight.*

He let his head sink into his hands. That had

felt good—too good. He might have wanted to do it for the better part of a decade, but all of his reasons for refraining were now flooding back to mind.

A brother didn't move in on his brother's ex-girlfriend, especially if that brother had already stated a renewed interest in her. Chet might have feelings for Mack, and that only made stepping back harder. Andy was also pretty testy right now as it was. There was more than his last family relationship to worry about; there was this ranch, which was already hanging in the balance…

Regardless of all the reasons against it, Chet didn't regret that kiss. It had been a long time coming, and even if it was the only kiss they'd ever share, he'd made it count. He might be the only principled man under sixty around here, but he *was* a man. Principles didn't change that.

Mackenzie shivered despite the warm night as she made her way across the dark turf toward her own land. The moon hung low in the sky, stars twinkling like spilled glitter, darkened here and there by tufts of clouds. Butter Cream trotted compliantly beside her and squeezed through the fence without so much as a bleat of protest.

Her lips tingled where his lips had pressed against them, and she could still feel his fingers in her hair, and she shivered again.

Wow. She'd had no idea that Chet Granger had that in him... He'd said he'd had feelings for her when they were kids, but this hadn't been a kiss rooted in the past. It was very much something from the present, and that made her nervous.

She breathed in the cool night air, and her mind went back to her conversation with her father. He'd said that Chet had been dead serious about buying her grandmother's land. Granny had mentioned it to Mack, too. But even with everything going against Chet—his brother threatening to sell to the developers, his being turned down for a loan big enough to buy his brother out—he hadn't once brought up the possibility of buying her land. Not once.

But why? That was the question. Why wouldn't he turn to the most obvious solution to his problem?

Unless Chet wasn't the last principled man under sixty. Maybe he was just like all the others—like her own father—capable of lies and deception when they got him what he wanted.

Even as she considered it, she didn't truly believe it. Chet wasn't like that, but there was something else holding her back, too. If she couldn't run this ranch on her own, she didn't believe that she had the right to continue depending on her neighbors. If she couldn't do this on her own, she needed to sell the place and find a business where she could stand on her own two feet. And when she'd asked Chet if she could run the ranch alone, he hadn't reassured her that she'd have no problem—he'd said that she could find someone else to guide her. And that wasn't what she'd been looking for—not that she'd had the chance to think it through all the way before he'd kissed her.

If she couldn't run this ranch by herself, then she needed to make the responsible decision and sell it. And if she couldn't stay in Hope, then she had no business kissing Chet or letting her feelings keep going in the direction they'd been moving. And she wasn't sure if she'd stay or not. While she wanted to make a success of this second chance her grandmother had afforded her, she had to be realistic. She wasn't sure how possible it truly was.

These Granger boys had a way of tying her up into knots, and it wasn't fair. When she'd last been on this ranch, it was Andy who'd tugged her into a romance that left her head spinning, and now Chet? She wasn't here to put her heart through the Granger wringer. She was here to try to build a life on the land her grandmother had left her.

None of the facts had changed since she'd arrived in Hope. Her land was still Chet's only solution to keeping his ranch, she still wasn't sure that she could run her ranch, and she still had the very difficult decision to make about what to do with her future. But one thing had changed... Dare she admit it? She was falling for him. That had changed, but the facts and the situation they found themselves in had not.

Feelings were not reliable enough to be a guide in life's toughest choices. Feelings flapped in the wind. She needed logic.

"I don't want this!" she said aloud as she ushered Butter Cream into her pen, then set down her kid. The goats looked up at her with their googly eyes, and Butter Cream let out a bleat. She sighed.

"Not you, Butter Cream," she said. She glanced at her watch. She'd have to be back in three hours to feed Chocolate Truffle her next bottle.

Mackenzie was no longer as certain about what had happened when Andy broke up with her back then, but there was one thing that she hadn't wavered about, and that was that Chet put his family first—always. What was best for the Grangers would always trump everything else. Including her. It always had. Logically speaking, there was no reason why Chet's designs on her grandmother's land should have changed.

"I should be careful," she whispered to herself. She didn't need anyone else's advice on that. She already knew it.

She shut off the light and closed the barn door, then headed with heavy steps toward the house. And as she strode across the stubby grass, a cool breeze lifting her hair away from her face, she suddenly knew exactly what she was feeling right now—in the midst of all those boiling emotions and uncertainties, she recognized one feeling as predominant: anger.

Just when she had gone and fallen for the rugged cowboy, she had to realize that soft kisses and a pounding heart didn't change facts. He was gentle and kind, gruff and determined, and when his lips met hers...

The memory of his kiss returned with surprising force, and she forced it back. It didn't matter how strong his hands were or how direct that gray gaze... That kiss wasn't fair! It was intense and warm, and it made her heart pound to even remember it, but it wasn't *fair*.

She trotted up the steps and let herself into the darkened mudroom of the ranch house. She was angry because she *wanted* to believe that Chet was falling for her the same way she was falling for him.

Except she'd conveniently forgotten along the way that Chet wanted the land, and he *would* offer to buy her out. Eventually, he'd have no other choice. He might not want to do it this way, but the developers had pushed up the land value, so he'd need someone willing to sell to him at the land's real cost. Did he have feelings for her? She'd felt it in his kiss—and Chet didn't strike her as that good an actor. But that didn't change the basic truth that the Grangers always stood together, and their land came first.

When it came down to the line, she wasn't going to win this.

Chapter 8

The next morning, Chet and Andy stood by the horse paddock after chores were done. The horses were already in the closest pasture, and Chet hooked his boot over the rail of the fence. The paddock was clean, and the dirt still retained the hoofprints. Chet pushed his hat back on his head. A brisk wind chilled his back where his shirt stuck to his sweaty skin. For once, Andy had gone out and worked as hard as Chet had, and Chet had a feeling that his brother was feeling a little bit bad about their argument the night before. They'd said a lot, but they hadn't talked about the right things—this land, their shared inheritance.

"Look, about last night," Chet said.

"Forget it." Andy pulled his hat off and slapped it against his leg. The sun was still low in the sky, the rays flooding Chet's arms and back with welcome warmth. The pinks and reds of sunrise had melted away, leaving a soft golden glow.

"No, really." Chet turned away again, unwilling to look his brother in the face while he talked about this. "It's your relationship. I'm sorry. I shouldn't have butted in."

Who was Chet to judge, anyway? He'd done something he shouldn't have in the barn last night. He could still remember the feeling of Mackenzie in his arms, but it was wrong. He shouldn't have gone there. A night's fitful sleep had convinced him of that.

Andy was silent for a moment. Then he sighed. "I meant it when I said I should have married Mackenzie."

Irritation swam up inside Chet's gut, and he glanced back toward his brother. "That was a long time ago. What makes you think she'd even be interested?"

Andy shrugged. "I don't know. We really had something at one time. It's hard to imagine that going away completely."

Chet could only hope that it had…except

that he wasn't really meaning to start anything up with Mack, either, so he knew that his emotions weren't steering him straight. If Mack wasn't going to stay, there was no point in putting himself through that kind of pain, not if they eventually had to part ways. If he ended up having to sell, then the result was the same. Besides, with his brother feeling things for Mack—things that made him want to punch the guy—then what kind of future was really possible between himself and Mackenzie? Any kind of future worth having included the rest of the family, too—including Andy.

And what if Andy got his way and was able to spark something up with Mackenzie again? Could Chet really step aside for the sake of family unity? He tried to picture it and came up with a ball of rage in the pit of his stomach. He'd been able to step back once when they were teens, but he didn't think he could repeat that kind of honorable sacrifice. Couldn't they both just leave her alone?

"What about Ida?" Chet asked quietly. "No judgment. I just want to know what happened."

Andy squinted against the morning sun. "We were just so different. I thought that it wouldn't matter, but it turns out that it did."

"Oh yeah?"

"She's so free-spirited. I thought that dating a yoga instructor would be hot, and it was, but…" Andy shrugged. "I always thought I'd end up with someone who could root me, tie me down."

"You hate being tied down," Chet said with a laugh. "So you want the actual ball and chain?"

"No… I don't know." Andy stuck his hat back onto his head. "It was the wedding—it changed her. All that pressure and stress. Everything costs, and there were all those expectations from both sides of the family, and—"

"You could have eloped," Chet said.

"No." Andy shook his head. "I know you think I'm just some flake, but that part matters to me. If I'm getting married, it's going to be in a church with all of our extended family to see it."

That took Chet by surprise. He'd never suspected that his brother felt so deeply about a wedding. Andy was the kind of man who liked flash and fun, not solemnity and church. And if family mattered that much to him, he certainly hoped it would factor in when it came to selling his pasture.

"And I'm broke." The last words came out low and flat.

There it was. He knew there had to be something more to this. Andy was good at making money, but he was also pretty good at spending it.

"I could have lent you some money," Chet said.

"No," Andy said. "I'm not ever going to owe you money."

Chet laughed softly. He'd expected that. He and Andy had never had an easy relationship, and he wasn't keen to lend his brother money, either. Cash had a way of making even the strongest family bonds awkward, and he wasn't sure his relationship with his brother could survive that.

"Is this why you want to sell the land?" Chet asked. "You need the cash?"

Andy was silent for a moment, then asked, "Do you know why dad gave you the house and me the pasture?"

Chet had never really considered the question too seriously before. He'd always assumed his father would set things up so he could run the place—it was a silent understanding between them that went back as far as those quiet mornings in the field together.

"I guess because I was the one who'd be running it," Chet said. "Makes sense."

"No. Because Dad didn't think I could be trusted to run the family business."

Chet regarded his brother in silence. Was there truth to that? He and Andy had both played their roles as they grew up—Chet learned the ranch and Andy fooled around. If Andy had wanted to inherit the ranch, why not pay a little more attention to the land earlier? Maybe their father would have seen some promise in him.

"Mom believed in me," Andy said. "She used to tell me that a ranch needed brawn and brains and sometimes they came in different packages. I think she thought of herself as the brains behind the ranch."

Chet smiled wistfully, remembering their mother. She'd been a countrywoman through and through, but she'd also been a reader. It was his mother who'd taught him to love books. They still had a few boxes of her books in the basement. His father had been the law around the ranch, showing them the right way to do things, and their mother had been the free spirit, finding creative ways to make things work. Maybe Andy had seen some of their mother in Ida, after all. The thought softened him.

"I miss Mom, too," he said quietly. "I think Dad left it to us like this because he wanted us to work together."

"Pipe dream there," Andy said with a short laugh.

"Yeah, maybe," Chet agreed. "But, Andy, I love this land. I can't just pick up and move somewhere else and have it be the same. I've got blood and sweat invested here."

"And what about my part of the inheritance?" Andy asked. "So I just walk away and let you ranch? What do I get out of this? Dad left me a hunk of land he never meant for me to touch. It pretty much amounts to cutting me out of the will."

"Let me buy you out," Chet said. "You know I can't match the offer you have on the table. I went to the bank to see what kind of loan I could get, and it's enough to pay you what the land was worth before that developer came on the scene."

Andy didn't answer for a second, and when he did, his voice was quiet. "I'll think about it, but you have to keep in mind that if I take the developer's offer, that's enough money to buy my own car dealership in Billings. I could own it. I wouldn't be beholden to anyone, and I'd be able to provide for me and—"

"Ida," Chet finished for him.

"—whomever I end up married to."

"So either I have the ranch or you have the

dealership," Chet said, bringing it back to the concrete once more.

"Something like that."

And there they were, backed against the wall again, with Andy holding all the power. Could he blame him for wanting to get all the money he could out of that land? It wasn't as if Andy had no plans for the cash—he wanted to buy his own business. That was the kind of dream that Chet could understand. For once, they seemed to be thinking the same way, except they couldn't both have their dreams at the same time.

"You should buy Mackenzie's land," Andy said after a moment. "Then I can sell mine. We'll both get what we want."

Mackenzie had asked him why he hadn't offered to buy her land the night before… Why was Andy suddenly bringing this up?

"Did you say anything about that to Mack?" he asked with a frown.

"And when exactly would I have had the chance with you standing guard?" his brother asked, then shook his head. "No, of course not. I'm saying it to you."

"Because she asked me why I hadn't offered to buy her out yet," Chet said.

"When?" Andy asked.

"Recently." He wasn't willing to talk about last night. Whatever else might happen, it belonged between him and Mack.

"And why haven't you offered to buy her out?" Andy asked. "It makes sense."

"When she first arrived, she told me she wanted to run the place," Chet said, although he knew that she wasn't as solid on that decision anymore. He was the one hoping she would stick it out.

"If she asked you about it, it's on her mind," his brother pointed out. "Besides, she's no ranching woman. She'll get tired of it soon enough. You'd better offer her a fair price before that developer does."

Chet glanced toward the barn where he'd pulled her close the night before. He felt heat rise in his neck as he remembered the sensation of her lips against his, and he looked quickly away. Her father had found her a good business opportunity in Billings, too, and she hadn't exactly turned him down flat. He was afraid right now that his brother was right. Pragmatically speaking, if he wanted to keep his ranch so badly, he should offer to buy out Mackenzie. He just couldn't bring himself to do it.

Chet pushed himself off the fence. He needed

to think this through on his own, get a grip on all these slippery loose ends. He wanted a strong cup of coffee and some silence. He started back toward the house, and his brother followed a half step behind. He was angry right now, because he hated having Andy hold this much control over his future, and he hated that Andy's idea sounded the most logical at the moment. If Mack wasn't really going to stay anyway, buying her land would give him the much-needed pasture.

When he'd kissed her, he'd wanted more from her than just friendship, but in the light of day, that didn't seem possible. Mack deserved better than to be toyed with, and if he had no serious intention of following through with his feelings, then he was obligated to keep those feelings to himself. So why couldn't he bring himself to offer to buy her land?

"I saw that the fair is back in town," Andy said.

Chet drew in a breath, attempting to clear out that heavy feeling inside him. It didn't work.

"Yeah, I noticed that." That fair was the place where teenagers got to break loose a little bit every summer. Chet had never spent a lot of time there, though. He'd been more concerned with the ranch. And truthfully, he'd never had a girl at the right time to take there. It only made him feel more alone walking solo among the couples.

"We should go," Andy said. "Like old times."

"What old times?" Chet replied with a laugh. "You went. I didn't go too often."

"Well, you should have. Make up for lost time." Andy grinned. "Get Mack to come, too. There's been too much tension around here lately."

"Is that a good idea?" Chet asked skeptically.

"We're all adults."

It had been ten years. All these stupid jealousies and this posturing needed to end. A lot of time had passed, and they were no longer hormonal teenagers. Maybe Andy was right. Besides, right now it looked as though Chet was the bigger threat to Mackenzie's peace of mind.

"Sure, I'll ask her if she's interested," Chet said. "Which reminds me, I need to head over there and help her out with the chores she can't do on her own yet."

"She has you doing her work, too?" Andy shook his head. "She still has you around her little finger?"

Chet suppressed a wince. How much had Andy guessed about his feelings for Mackenzie back then? He'd been careful to hide them, but then, Andy was always a little more perceptive behind that dumb grin than he let on.

"I'm being neighborly," he replied shortly.

Andy arched an eyebrow.

"Worried about me?" Chet joked, enjoying his brother's momentary discomfort. It wasn't often that he had the upper hand when it came to a woman, even if he was the only one who knew about it.

Andy rolled his eyes and ambled off toward the house without another word, but Chet was left with that uncomfortable knot in his gut.

It was degrading, mostly. He'd been pining for his younger brother's girl, and no man took pride in that. The only comfort he'd had was in thinking that he'd at least been able to keep that little shameful fact to himself.

"Blast it," he muttered, and he set his hat back on his head and headed toward Mackenzie's land. That kiss wasn't going to go anywhere, and the best thing he could do was to put it behind them. He'd have to face her sooner or later, and he might as well start now.

Mackenzie eyed the bales of hay that sat just inside the back door of the barn. Dust motes hung in the slanting morning sunlight, and the smell of hay filled her with memories. As a teenager, the hay bales had been an ideal place to sit and think. She used to sit out here in a pair of cutoff jean shorts and a tank top and stare out through the open sliding door at the property. Mackenzie glanced behind her. The winding dirt road was the same, as were the rolling plains that stretched out toward the horizon, but it was different now. Now the scene represented responsibility and work. This was no vacation.

"What was Granny thinking?" she asked herself aloud.

There had to be better family members to leave the land to—her father being the most obvious, or one of her uncles or aunts. There had to be someone who could have been trusted not to sell out. If her grandmother had cared about this land at all, why would she leave it to the one granddaughter who had no clue?

Mackenzie remembered one day the summer that her parents got divorced when a calf had died, and Mackenzie hadn't taken it well. She'd sat down and cried on the ground next to the still body. It wasn't only the calf. She'd wept for everything that she'd lost—her parents' marriage, her security, her sense of certainty that all was right with the world—and for the little calf who hadn't been strong enough to make it.

"The Lord gives, and the Lord takes away," Granny had murmured softly.

"That doesn't help, Granny!" Mackenzie had snapped.

Granny then squatted down next to her on the ground and said the words that would bring Mackenzie through her parents' divorce and all the other disappointments that life would throw at her.

"There's a lot of giving and a lot of taking," Granny said thoughtfully. "Your parents—your dad, mainly—took something away from you that you needed, but you have to find a way to participate still."

"In my parents' divorce?" she asked incredulously.

"Maybe not the actual divorce, but you'd better find a way to participate in putting together that new life you'll all be living. You'd better get in there and start making your voice heard. This is going to be your new life, too."

Mackenzie suspected that that participation was what Granny had given her in this ranch—because ranches didn't run on thoughts and theories. They ran on sweat and blisters—she was quickly finding that out—and as she looked out over that winding dirt road and the fields that stretched out beyond, she saw not only work and responsibility, but a demand. The land and the livestock required something more of her—her physical and mental participation in the running of this ranch.

If she was going to keep this place, she was going to need to hire some workers, buy more cattle and start making a profit. There was no way around it. She was either all in or she had to sell.

The sound of footsteps drew her attention just as Chet came around the corner. He pulled his hat off, ran a hand through his hair, then dropped the hat back in place with a slow smile.

"Morning," he said.

"Good morning." She smiled hesitantly. This was the first time she'd seen him since that kiss, and she wasn't sure what to expect. His gray eyes moved away from her to the bales of hay and her pickup truck with the tailgate down, and without another word, he stepped forward, grabbed a bale by the twine and hoisted it up.

Chet was a strong man—Mackenzie couldn't lift a bale on her own—and he walked it over to the truck. A vein popped on his forearm as he tossed the bale into the bed of the truck. Then he turned back to the barn and heaved up another bale of hay. This job sure was easier with some brawn around, she had to admit.

"Thanks," she said as he lobbed a second one beside the first, then brushed his hands off on his jeans.

"No problem." He hooked a thumb toward the truck. "Filling the feeder in the pasture?"

There was a large iron feeder in the smaller pasture, since the smaller enclosure didn't always have enough space to properly feed the livestock on grass alone.

"I seem to remember doing that when I visited here." She suddenly had a sense of misgiving.

"No, it's a good call." He put a hand on the hood of the pickup. "Need a hand?"

"Yeah." She glanced at him, feeling a blush rise in her cheeks. "Thanks."

She was thinking of their kiss in spite of her best efforts. It irritated her that Chet had been so memorable. If only he'd been sloppy or awkward—easier to brush off as a bad idea—but he hadn't been.

Mackenzie got into the driver's seat and Chet hopped in next to her. She stole a look at him as she turned the key—his stubble softening the hard lines of his chin. She didn't say anything more as they lurched forward and headed down the dusty road.

"Are we going to talk about this?" Chet asked after a moment of silence.

Mackenzie stepped on the gas and inwardly grimaced. They'd have to, but she wasn't even sure what to say. Alone last night, it had been so clear that Chet was looking out for his own ends, but with him here in the truck with her, it seemed different again.

"I don't have anything to say," she admitted.

"Okay, well—" he pulled off his hat and sat it on his knee "—I do. I'm sorry."

"For what part, exactly?" she asked.

"For all of that." He caught her eye, then gave her a tentative smile. "Look, I told you before that I'd had feelings for you when you were dating my brother, but it was more than that. I had a pretty wild crush on you. It was embarrassing. Kind of stupid."

Embarrassing and *stupid* weren't exactly the words every woman wanted to hear.

He pulled a hand through his hair and looked out the window. "And I guess I'd been wanting to do that for a long time."

The memory of his strong hand moving through the back of her hair brought a shiver.

"How come you never said anything back then?" Mackenzie asked.

"You were Andy's girl," he said, as if it were the most obvious thing in the world. "Brothers don't do that."

"Actually, a lot do."

"You said I was the last principled man under sixty," he said. "I guess I was back then, too."

She wished she'd known then the way Chet had felt. If she'd known that Chet had been interested, it might have changed whom she'd dated. Chet had caught her attention first because of his stoic strength. He was quiet, controlled. Maybe too controlled, because she'd never suspected that he'd felt anything more than friendship for her.

But maybe wondering about all of this was stupid, too. It didn't change Chet's loyalty to the family, and it certainly didn't change the current complications. What he felt for her all those years ago didn't much matter when they were all adults with adult responsibilities. Summers no longer seemed as if they lasted forever. And not everything was possible.

"I guess so," she said. "Well, it was a long time ago…"

"Definitely. A very long time ago."

She shot him a glance as she turned toward

the pasture, and truthfully, it didn't feel so long ago right now looking at him, but this was the problem with the Granger boys. They'd always had a way of catching her off balance and she needed to put an end to that. It was hard to be a full participant in your life when you were always being swept off by some current.

Mackenzie pulled to a stop and pushed open her door.

"So that kiss was just…" She turned back. She needed the clarification on this. "That was just for old times' sake, then?"

He considered for a moment. "No. But I should have left it in the past."

Great. So he'd kissed her, remembering how he'd felt all those years ago, and she'd found herself a flustered mess for a guy who wasn't even attracted to her once he'd had some time to think about it. Maybe the reality of a grown woman with emotional baggage and not a lot of ranching know-how was less appealing upon some careful reflection. She wouldn't entirely blame him.

"Okay." She got out of the truck and slammed the door harder than necessary.

Mack headed around the back of the truck. This was another excellent reason to keep her emotional distance from Chet Granger, and she hauled open the tailgate, fully willing to hoist that bale on her own just to vent her frustration. Chet slammed his door shut and came around beside her.

"Move," Chet said, and while his tone was gruff, his eyes were gentle.

"Excuse me?" she shot back.

"Move," he repeated, then cracked a smile. "Don't give yourself a hernia because I'm an ass."

He had a good point there, and she stepped aside, allowing him to lift out the first bale. He carried it to the gate, and she opened the latch and let him through to the feeder. She followed. It didn't take long for him to fill the feeder with the two bales, and when he was done, they arranged the hay so that the cows could reach it more easily. After they finished, he studied her, uncertainty swimming in those gray eyes.

"Look," he said quietly.

"Never mind," she said with a brisk shake of her head. She didn't need any more reassurances—they weren't working, anyway.

"Hey." His tone grew firmer. "Mack, I don't want to ruin our friendship. I'm sorry. My feelings aren't your problem, and I should have reined all that in last night."

When she looked up at him, she found his gaze still fixed intently on her. He was truly sorry—she could see that much. But he was taking a lot for granted about that kiss—namely that she'd never experienced another one like it. Of course, she hadn't, but that wasn't the point here.

"It's okay, Chet," she said with a small smile. "I'm a grown woman. It isn't like I've never been kissed before."

Chet's face broke into a grin and he shook his head. "Touché."

They walked together back to the gate as the cows came closer to check out their new source of food. Chet pulled the gate open and motioned Mackenzie through first.

"So we're friends still?" he asked, closing it behind him and securing the clasp.

"Of course." She swept a hand through her hair, dragging it back over her shoulders.

He paused for a moment, then squinted as if trying to decide something.

"Then what would you think of getting out tonight?" he asked. "As friends, of course. The fair is in town, and it might be nice to let loose for a few hours. Andy's coming, too, just in case you don't want to hang out with me alone all evening."

Mackenzie raised her eyebrows and considered. It would be nice to get away from it all for a few hours. As much as she was enjoying working Granny's land, she could feel the exhaustion setting in, too.

"Sure," she agreed. "That would be nice."

The three of them hanging out again—it was almost a relief after that kiss. She wasn't sure that she'd trust herself wandering through fairgrounds with Chet in the dusk, but adding Andy into the mix brought it all back into innocent fun.

"Great." Chet smiled ruefully and headed for the truck. "Because there's been a wildfire of gossip about us, and we should probably clear some of that up."

"By being seen out together at the fair?" she asked, baffled.

"You bet." He hauled open the truck door. "What better way to prove that there's nothing to talk about?"

Chapter 9

That evening, Chet and Andy pulled up in front of Mackenzie's house in Chet's slightly beat-up old Chevy. It had seen better days, but the truck was still reliable and it drove like an old friend. Chet was driving and Andy sat in the passenger seat. Andy had put more care than usual in his appearance, his shirt open at the neck and a large titanium-cased watch falling outside his sleeve. He'd made good money in Billings, and it showed in his dress. Chet, on the other hand, wore his good jeans—the ones he wore to church—and a clean blue button-up shirt and his good cowboy hat. He was clean, shaven and smelling appropriate. The rest of his good looks, he was born with.

Mack waved from the front window and a minute later came out the door. He tried not to look too closely at her formfitting jeans as she turned to lock the door, and when she turned back toward them, a pink embroidered blouse draped down just far enough to expose the curve of her collarbone. That long hair hung loose and free down her shoulders, the wind ruffling it, and she had to pull it away from her face as she approached the truck. It had been a long time since he'd stared at Mackenzie like that. She was still stunning, and he was still feeling more than he should be.

"Get in the back, Andy."

Andy narrowed his eyes at his brother, but he got out and held the door for Mackenzie as she climbed up into the truck, and Chet didn't miss the direction of his brother's appreciative gaze as she did so. When she reached for the door to close it, he opened the back door and hopped up.

"Hi, guys," Mack said as she tugged at her seat belt. "Sorry to dethrone you, Andy."

"Hey, anything for a lady," Andy said with a laugh that irritated Chet just a little.

They weren't supposed to be competing

for her, but Chet couldn't help that twinge of competition inside him. Mackenzie smelled good—that mixture of shampoo and something floral that Chet had always associated with her. She brushed some dried dirt off the side of her jeans.

"I gave Chocolate Truffle one last bottle before I left," she said with a small shrug.

He couldn't quite explain how his heart did an extra thump at that. Mack had never been very country, but she seemed to have figured out the priorities, at least. Animals first. Clean jeans second. Chet put the truck into gear and pulled away from the house, tires crunching against gravel as he headed up the drive toward the dirt road.

"I think I took you to this fair on our first date, didn't I?" Andy said from the backseat as Chet eased onto the dirt road.

Chet was tempted to say something smart-alecky, but he kept it to himself. The fair used to be a favorite spot for his brother to take girls he dated. Mackenzie turned, her golden hair shining in the evening sunlight that spilled through the windshield, and looked at Andy quizzically.

"No, you took me there just before we broke up. What happened that night, anyway?"

Chet glanced in the rearview mirror and caught Andy's frozen smile. Mackenzie shifted her attention to Chet next, and he winced. Andy was embarrassed about his teenage shenanigans. Maturity had changed him, and as far as Chet knew, Andy had been faithful to the women in his life ever since. But Mack was staring at Chet now.

"Ask Andy," he said. It wasn't his sin to reveal.

"I'm serious, Andy," she said, glancing over her shoulder. "What happened? Everything was perfect, and then you just disappeared on me. Thank God Chet found me and brought me home, but it always bothered me."

"I—uh—" Andy laughed uncomfortably. "I don't even remember."

Chet remembered the episode clearly, even if his brother was having some selective amnesia. Andy had met up with the girl who would be his next girlfriend, and she'd asked him to go do something with her. That was when Chet had gotten that slightly tense phone call from his brother asking him to do him just one favor... Andy had been starting with someone new, with a little overlap.

"The thing is," Chet said, his words measured and low, "if a guy really cares, he's there. No way around it."

Andy's face hardened into a look of anger in the rearview, and Chet ignored it. It was the truth. Andy might have recognized what a great catch Mack was, but he hadn't loved her—not the way he should have. When a guy fell for a girl, he didn't get sidetracked with someone else, and he didn't pawn her off on his brother.

Andy had asked Chet to pick up Mack from the fair and to cover for him. Chet had done that. In fact, he'd been eager to go and get her, but he'd been reluctant about the covering part. He could still remember the confused look on her face when he found her by the Ferris wheel. Mackenzie had been tearstained and upset, and he could tell she sensed something was wrong. She cared more for Andy than he did for her— it had to hurt. Appreciating a woman's worth and falling in love with her could come at the same time, but they didn't always. It was possible for a man to see exactly how wonderful a woman was and still not be in love. And Andy hadn't been.

"You saying I didn't care?" Andy snapped.

"It was almost a decade ago," Chet replied,

eyeing his brother with a direct glance in the mirror. "Let it go."

The truth was, ten years ago, they had been kids still. They'd been playing with emotions that were new to all of them, but time had changed them all. Ten years ago, they were all full of potential and their whole lives were ahead of them, and now they were solidly set on their life paths. A crush on a seventeen-year-old girl wasn't the same thing as realizing that you were falling hard for a grown woman. This wasn't about fantasy or potential; it was about reality and choices. Mack might have been exciting back then, but right now she occupied a deeper place in his heart. He truly liked the woman she'd grown into. He liked how hard she worked, her determination to run a ranch she knew little about. And she was eerily wise, able to see beyond his words to his emotions boiling beneath. That was something he knew better than to take for granted. Most women complained about his reluctance to open up, but Mack seemed to get beyond that without much effort on her part. She knew her mind, and she didn't get derailed by anyone else's opinions, either. Mackenzie Vaughn had matured into an amazing woman. The man

who won her heart would be lucky for a life-
time, but her heart was carefully protected.

"Well, you were a sweetheart to drive out
and pick me up," Mack said, smiling in Chet's
direction. "It was late, and I was a teary mess.
I'm sure that was the last place you wanted to
be."

She was dead wrong there. He'd been the
tiniest bit glad to see his brother's interest in
Mackenzie waning, and when he'd driven out
there to pick her up, he'd been both irritated at
his brother for being a moron and a little excited at the chance of being alone with her. The
whole ride back she'd tried to hold back her
tears, and he hadn't blamed her. When they finally got back and he'd dropped her off in front
of her grandmother's house, she'd told him she
wasn't ready to be alone yet and asked if he
wanted to talk. That night, he had wrapped his
arms around her for the first time and held her
close while she sniffled into his shirt. Wild
horses couldn't have dragged him away.

"Nah," he said with a shrug. "It was fine."

"Do you remember how we sat outside Granny's barn that night and talked and talked? I
was so mad at Andy, and you weren't ready
to go home…" Mack paused. "I think you told

me about treating foot-and-mouth disease or something."

Chet laughed out loud. "Yeah, that sounds about right."

He hadn't been exactly smooth at the ripe old age of nineteen, and he'd been desperate to keep her there with him. He'd had to say something, and he couldn't say what had been uppermost in his mind—that he was a better choice than his brother, that he'd never leave her out there standing by herself next to a Ferris wheel, and that if he had the chance that night, he wanted to kiss her. The chance hadn't come—or maybe he hadn't had the deftness to make it happen. Regardless, he'd eventually walked her back to her grandmother's house and she'd disappeared inside, and Chet had lain awake that night, remembering how she'd felt when she'd cried in his arms.

"Always the gentleman," Mack said with a smile, and Chet wasn't sure he liked that easy sound to her voice when she said those words. He might have been a gentleman—he might still be a gentleman—but that didn't cancel out the fact that he was also a man. Just because he knew how to treat a woman right didn't mean he was castrated—he'd made that clear enough in the barn the other night.

They were approaching the town of Hope now, and he slowed to the speed limit as they cut through. The fairgrounds were just on the other side of town, and in the distance he could see the very tips of some of the rides.

Being with Mack at the fair would have been perfect if it weren't for his brother along for the ride, but then, it was probably better to have Andy around. Andy lent a bit of reality to the situation, a living and breathing reminder of why Chet had to step carefully.

The parking lot for the fairgrounds wasn't big enough, so the extra vehicles flowed over into an empty field beside it, a stretch of pickup trucks, SUVs and cars from town. A few RVs were parked at the far end of the lot—possibly for the carnies working the fair. Chet pulled into a grassy space and turned off the engine. He came around the side of the vehicle next to Mackenzie, drinking in that distant popcorn scent of the fair.

"You bought me deep-fried pickles."

Mack's voice was close and low, and he looked over at her in surprise. "Pardon?"

"Back then," she said. "You bought me those battered deep-fried pickle slices, remember? And we ate them together on the drive back."

That was right. Every time it looked as

though she'd give in to those tears, he'd nudged the box closer to her and said, *These are better than Andy*. She'd smiled at his little joke, and he'd felt like a hero.

"Yeah, I'd forgotten about that," he said. "I'll get you more tonight," he said with a grin. "And whatever other junk food you'll eat. Tonight is on me."

The fair hadn't changed much in the past ten years. The lowering sun was close to setting, sending rays out from behind the rides and tents. The sounds of games and attention grabbers jangled discordantly, and through it all the scent of popcorn and deep-fried everything permeated the air. The ground was dusty and dry, and as the three of them stepped onto the fairgrounds, Mackenzie put her hands into her pockets.

"It's the same," she said.

"It's only been ten years," Chet replied with a quick laugh. "Takes longer than that to change anything around here."

Mackenzie had to admit to the wisdom in his words, but it applied to more than traveling carnivals and local businesses. Too much had stayed the same around here, so much so that standing at the fair with the Granger brothers was so familiar that it hurt.

"Hey, Andy!" a man called out. He wore a cowboy hat and had a thumb hooked in a belt loop.

"Dwight!" Andy grinned in the other man's direction and sauntered over, leaving Mackenzie and Chet to themselves. Obviously, the two men knew each other well, because there was a lot of laughing and backslapping.

"Who's that?" Mackenzie asked.

"Friend from high school." Chet glanced at his brother again. "We might as well go take a look around. Andy will be a bit."

Mack nodded, and they moved off toward the blinking lights of the games and attractions, Chet feeling solid and comforting next to her. It was tempting to slip her hand into his, but she knew better. It hadn't been like this the last time she'd seen Chet at the fair. That had been a dismal night and he'd been protective and sweet. As she walked next to Chet now, the atmosphere was charged with something deeper, something she wished she could explore a little bit, but that didn't mean that it would last. This was the kind of evening to enjoy, tuck away into her memory and appreciate it for what it was: a nice night with a good man.

"Do you want a deep-fried pickle?" Chet asked.

The smell of oil and batter floated to them over a warm breeze, and while the sky was growing duskier, the lights around them seemed to brighten.

"Sure." She grinned up at him. "Are they still as good?"

Better than Andy. That was how he'd described them, hadn't he? It still amused her.

"I guess we'll find out."

The little hut didn't have a lineup, and Chet stepped up to order, peeling a couple of bills off a roll from his pocket. He was strong, confident. Would things have turned out differently if she'd dated Chet instead of Andy back then? It was hard to tell. Ten years had changed her as well as Chet, and she wouldn't trade in her college degree or life experience, either. It was bittersweet, because standing here in the fragrant air of the county fair, she knew what she had to do. She just didn't want to do it. Hope had moved on without her, no matter how much Chet protested to the contrary, and she had moved on, too.

When the food was ready, Chet passed her

chips sending up an aroma that made her stomach growl.

"It matters to me," she said, and right now, she needed to take care of herself.

"Andy called me up and asked me to come get you," he said simply. "So I did."

"But why?" she asked. "Where did he disappear to?"

Chet opened a packet of tartar sauce and squeezed it onto the box lid, then dipped a chip into it and popped it into his mouth.

"You should probably ask Andy that," he said.

"I did," she retorted. "You were there. He didn't answer me."

This whole male protectiveness thing was getting old quickly.

"Hey." His voice was low and strong, and his gaze pinned her to the spot. "I'm a man of my word, and that means you can count on it, too. So don't ask me to break a promise, Mack. You know I'm not that kind of guy."

She didn't answer him. Maybe she was being unrealistic expecting to sort this all out before she left.

"I can tell you this," he said quietly. "Trust your gut, Mack."

That was what she was doing by asking all

these questions—listening to that uncertain feeling deep inside that told her there was more to this. But a gut feeling could take a woman only so far, and eventually someone had to spill already. His words sounded faintly like a warning, though.

"Trust my gut with whom, exactly?" she asked, shooting him a wry smile. "That's rather vague."

"All of us." He pulled his gaze away from her and he put his attention back into the food in front of him.

Was that a warning? She had no idea, but his words felt heavy with meaning. The Grangers stood together, and the Grangers needed land. Why was it that she kept hoping that this was about something more, something deeper? She hadn't come to Hope to find romance. She hadn't even come for answers about the past, yet here she was.

Stupid, she mentally chided herself. When a man told you to be cautious of him, it was for good reason.

The sound of chatting people eating their greasy fair food murmured around them, but Mackenzie and Chet sat in silence for a long while. It was as though she'd come up against a wall with Chet, and she knew better than to pound on it. He wouldn't tell her what she wanted to know, and that was most telling itself. After a few minutes of munching on their food, Chet's low voice broke the silence.

"Our mom took us to the fair when we were kids."

Mack could hear a difference in his voice. His tone was quiet, and she had to lean closer to hear him clearly.

"I tried to win her a teddy bear and spent all my allowance in the attempt. It was a water-gun game where I was supposed to knock down a bottle."

Chet didn't talk about his mother often, and the tenderness in his voice gave her pause.

"That's rather sweet."

"I felt like an idiot when I lost again and again," Chet went on. "And that night, I went to bed miserable because I hadn't been able to win the bear for her. She came into my room and I still remember how she looked standing in the doorway." He let out a sigh. "She told me that she didn't need a teddy bear to know how much I loved her. She said she could see it every day in how hard I worked. I felt like a real man that night. I was taking care of her."

"How old were you then?" she asked.

"Maybe fourteen." He sighed again. "But

Andy spent more time with her than I did. He'd come inside and talk to her while I was out with the animals. When she got sick, I tried to spend more time with her, and that's when I saw how close she and Andy were."

"You were jealous?" Mackenzie asked.

"Yeah, I guess so." He jabbed his fork into the cardboard box. "But that teddy bear had mattered to me. I'd just found out that my mom had cancer, and I couldn't even win her a bear."

Mackenzie felt the tears well up in her eyes. "I'm sure she understood how much you wanted to."

He nodded slowly. "Yeah."

"And those games are rigged, you know."

"I know." He shrugged. "In life, most of them are. But sometimes a guy thinks that if he just has heart enough, he can beat the toughest odds."

"How old were you when she died?" she asked quietly.

"Fifteen."

Mackenzie slipped her arm through his. "I'm sure she tried to stick around for you boys, too. Sometimes heart isn't enough."

"Sometimes," he agreed gruffly, and he met her gaze. "But I'm the kind of guy who keeps hoping that this time it might be." His gray eyes moved over her face slowly, his chiseled features softening until she thought she could see a glimpse of the nineteen-year-old in him again. He ran a rough hand over hers where it rested on his biceps.

"I wish you'd told me how you felt back then," she said quietly.

"Would you have ditched my brother and chosen the serious party pooper instead?" he asked with a chuckle. He looked away, his gaze moving over the far tables.

Would she have? Perhaps not. Ten years ago, she'd lacked the wisdom she had now. Ten years ago, Andy had seemed exciting and Chet had been exasperating. Now that she was a grown woman, it was the other way around.

"Oh, Chet," she said softly. "I was young and stupid back then. Who's to say what I would have done and lived to regret?"

Chet traced her fingers one by one with the tip of his middle finger. "There was this one afternoon you were in the hayloft reading a book. I came by to get a tool your granny had borrowed from us, and you hadn't heard me come in. I watched you read for I don't know how long. You were gorgeous—like always. The sun was coming through the open loft door, and you were propped up on a hay bale, your legs crossed in front of you… I had to physically stop myself from climbing on up and showing you exactly how I felt about you."

A memory of his hands moving through her hair, his lips coming down onto hers, brought a blush to her cheeks. Her breath caught in her throat, and for a moment she thought he might lean closer and show her exactly what he meant, but he didn't. His finger kept up the slow tracing over each of hers, moving from knuckle to fingertip in a patient glide.

"I wish you had," she said at last.

"Imagining something and doing it are two different things," he said quietly. "Besides, I made some noise and you looked down and saw me. You immediately asked me where Andy was."

His finger stopped tracing hers as those words came out of his mouth and her heart sank in her chest. She remembered that afternoon. She'd been too moon-eyed over Andy by that point to ever notice his older brother. If only she'd been able to look a little wider back then. But she'd been loyal, too, and by then she'd made her choice in Andy.

"You asked me what happened at the fair that night," he said. "Do you really want to know?"

Chapter 10

Looking over at Mackenzie, her honey-blond hair tucked behind one ear so that her milky neck drew his eye, he knew what he was going to do—even if he did regret it later.

"If I tell you, Mack," he said quietly, "I'd appreciate it if you didn't let Andy know that I've told you. I'd rather not tick him off right now with that developer sweet-talking him, if you know what I mean."

Mackenzie turned toward him, those blue eyes fixed on his face hopefully. He had a feeling that expression was going to change when she heard the truth, though, and he hoped he wasn't going to be the cause of more grief than necessary.

"Of course," she said. "I'm a woman of my word, too, you know."

"Yeah, I know, it's just…" He sighed. "It wasn't Andy who asked me to keep the secret. It was Helen."

Mack's eyes widened, and a voice came over the loudspeaker, interrupting him. "Would the owner of the blue Chevy pickup, license plate number—" here there was a rustle of papers, and then the number was rattled off "—please return to your vehicle. The lights are on."

The timing was impeccable. Chet closed his eyes and blew out a breath. That was his truck. He didn't remember having the lights on, but he must have flicked them on without even thinking. His truck battery wasn't the strongest and could use changing soon, so if he didn't get those lights off pronto, it would drain completely and they wouldn't be getting home tonight. It was just lucky someone had noticed.

"That's mine," he said. "Sorry. You stay here and eat. Save my spot. I'll be back in ten minutes."

"Wait, you can't just walk away. You were telling me—" she started. "Never mind. I'll come along."

"No, stay." He cleared his throat. "Seriously. I'll be back in ten minutes. And then I'll fill you in. That's a promise."

Chet would tell her—he'd just given his word that he would—but he wanted a couple of minutes to order his thoughts. If he was about to break an oath to a deceased friend, then he should at least make sure he did it carefully.

He rose to his feet, easing his long legs out from under the picnic table. This wasn't the kind of thing he could just blurt out and walk away from. He'd need to gauge how she was taking it and maybe talk her through it a bit. That took time.

As Chet headed for the parking lot, his mind was swirling. He hated this balance of self-interest and morality. He wasn't even sure if he could call telling Mack the truth the moral thing to do, because he'd be breaking a promise to her late grandmother in the process. This was a whole murky gray area, and he hated gray. He liked black-and-white. He liked to know exactly what side of the fence he was on.

"Idiot," he muttered to himself. He had excellent reasons to keep his mouth shut, and in a moment of weakness with those snapping blue eyes riveted to his face, he was about to go against everything he'd been so sure about mere days earlier.

He obviously wasn't thinking straight right now, and he wasn't even sure that he cared. Mackenzie deserved something better, and maybe it was stupid of him, but he wanted to be that something better for her—or a part of it, if that was all he could manage. If Andy sold, he might be forced out, too. At least her memories of the Grangers wouldn't be all heartbreak.

A quilt display stood next to a Girl Scouts tent selling cookies. The display was set up on racks, a few quilts hung by clamps to larger frames so that the full pattern could be seen by passersby. The Hope quilting guild made tiny quilts to be given out to new mothers as they left the hospital, as well as slightly larger quilts for a children's hospital in Billings. But after the charitable work was done, those ladies worked their fingers to the bone for the quilt competition at the fair. He knew this because Helen had competed yearly.

As he passed the quilt display, one of the tags caught his eye. He hadn't been paying attention the first time they'd passed that way, and his heart sank. It was affixed to a pinwheel quilt made of pink and orange—bright and attractive. He remembered seeing Helen working on this on her porch, stitching each piece together by hand, her knuckles swelling with the meticulous work. But she'd always been the tough type, and she'd said there was a right way and a wrong way to make a quilt. For Helen, the right way was with hand stitching.

This particular quilt had a sign pinned at the top saying Honorable Mention: Quilt by Helen Vaughn.

Helen must have submitted this quilt to the contest six months ago, and the realization that she'd not lived long enough to see it win an honorable mention was sad. Helen had had a lot more living to do, and she'd been taken far too soon. But standing here, looking at her quilt hanging in front of him, he felt a tickle of guilt.

He was about to break his word, when his word was all she'd needed from him because she'd known that of all men, Chet Granger could be trusted to stand by it.

"Helen, I'm sorry," he muttered aloud. Either way he stepped, it looked as if he was hurting Mack, and he hated that. He just wanted to ease some of that pain for her, except he couldn't tell what would help most—his silence or the truth. Helen's bet was on silence. Here's hoping that he was right and the truth would set her free—

stories and proverbs. Mack had to do this one on her own.

"Hey, you."

Mackenzie startled and looked up to see Andy standing behind her, and he shot her a warm smile—the kind she remembered from a decade ago.

"Hi, Andy," she said. "I didn't hear you come up."

"I'm sneaky that way." He winked and she found herself grinning in spite of herself. He angled his head toward the rides. "Want to walk with me?"

"Chet just had to go turn off the lights of the truck, and he'll be back in a minute—"

"Yeah, the truck." Something flickered across Andy's face. Then he shrugged. "Chet is a big boy now. I'm sure he can find us. It's not exactly the world's fair. Besides, I wanted to talk to you. Alone. Chet's been looming lately."

This fair was small and intimate—not exactly a great place to get lost. She was sure Chet could find them easily enough, and she was finished with her food, anyway. Besides, Chet wouldn't finish what he was telling her until they were alone again.

"All right," she said. "Let's walk a little bit."

With any luck, Andy would run into another old friend by the time Chet came back.

Mackenzie picked up the last of her food and closed the container, then got to her feet and angled toward the big garbage. She looked toward the main gates as they came away from the table, but there was no sign of Chet.

"So how are you liking working the ranch?" Andy asked.

"It's—" She smiled. "It's hard."

"Do you miss city life yet?" he asked.

"Sometimes," she admitted. "At least I got weekends off."

She laughed at her own little joke, but there was sadness underneath it. She'd miss Hope, and she'd miss Granny's ranch, but it wasn't the same without Granny and she couldn't base her future on the help of neighbors. She could either do this alone or face facts.

"Why not go back?" Andy asked. "I had no idea you were so close by. If I'd known—"

"You were engaged, Andy," she reminded him.

"Yeah. So I wouldn't have." He shrugged. "It's good to see you again, though. Really good."

Mackenzie crossed her arms in front of her as they made their way out into the general mix of people. A ringtoss game had drawn a few people, and one teenager seemed to be doing pretty well at it. Every time a ring landed, a trill of chimes erupted from the speakers. Everyone was watching the kid throw, and they sidled around the outside of the crowd.

"Mack…" Andy dipped his head closer to her. "I wanted to talk to you about something."

A family wandered past them pushing a double stroller with two toddlers inside. They were both blond-haired boys with grubby faces. Mack stepped aside to give them room, and Andy trailed her. They moved around the corner from the ringtoss. The vendors were calling out to passersby, and the jangly music of the game grated on Mackenzie's nerves.

"Oh?" She shot him a curious look. "What about?"

"Chet."

Andy scanned the people moving from tent to tent, and then he tugged her into an empty space between the ringtoss booth and another tent selling T-shirts and knickknacks. Mackenzie followed, her intrigue heightened. It was dusk, and in the causeway, lights illuminated everything as bright as noon. But here between the tents, they stood in the shadows.

"What's the matter?" she asked, frowning.

"I don't even know how to start." He smiled awkwardly. "I know you probably think I'm the problem here. I swoop back into town and threaten to sell my land, but—"

"Don't do it," Mackenzie said. "He's your brother."

"I have to do it," he said with a sigh. "If I don't, I'm walking away from my inheritance, because I'm not staying here. My life is in Billings. I suspect yours is, too."

There was truth in that, and it pricked her at her heart. He was right. Her life was in Billings, and even if she didn't much like the choices she'd made there, Hope wasn't going to be home, sweet home. Things had to change, but Hope wasn't her answer.

"I'm not sure I'm cut out for this," she admitted. "I don't like to take something on that I can't finish on my own."

"I thought so," he said. "And there's no shame in that. So have you thought of who you'll sell to?"

Mackenzie's heart sped up and she looked out toward the crowds of people. The family with the stroller was beside a concession stand. The mother was wiping one of the toddler's noses, and the father was paying for some Popsicles. The woman paused and glanced up and she and her husband exchanged a smile. They looked tired, and they weren't exactly dressed to impress, but that look they exchanged appeared to be something really precious, and one day, when she was dressed in mom clothes and feeling tired, she hoped she had a husband who still looked at her like that. Until then, she needed to take care of herself.

"I've been thinking about it," Andy went on. "And just hear me out. I can't leave my brother in the lurch. I've been trying to talk to him about selling, and he won't do it. He's stubborn—you know that. He wants this land, and he won't be happy otherwise."

"You want me to sell my ranch to him," she concluded, and she realized with a sick feeling that this was it… This was the proposal she'd been waiting for the past couple of weeks. It was coming—she'd felt it in her bones—but she hadn't expected it to come from Andy. She raised her eyes to meet Andy's steady gaze.

"So who is this coming from?" she asked. "You or Chet?"

"I'm saying it, but you know what he wants deep down," Andy replied with a bitter smile. "What are brothers for?"

She stood in silence, his words sinking in. Maybe it was more complicated for Chet, given his feelings for her, but Andy was right. Chet might not want to say it, but it was the obvious solution staring them all in the face.

"I haven't thought it through all the way," she admitted.

"Fair enough," he said, nodding. "But I'm running out of time here. I need to sign, or the deal is off the table. I'd hate to miss out on it. Chet won't ask you, but I will. Would you at least consider selling to my brother?"

"The Grangers looking out for each other," she said sourly. Nothing had changed. She had fallen for one of them, and the other was rising up in defense of him. They were a family, one that made her feel so jealous of their loyalty she wanted to cry. That kind of loyalty was what she'd been aching for the past ten years, and here it was—always just out of reach.

"We always do." There was an apology in his tone, as if he sensed the unfairness of it all. "Mack, I'm sorry. I can't put it off any longer. I want to buy the car dealership I'm currently managing, and I want to move forward. The money from the developers is the only way to do it." He paused and caught her gaze. "And if you're in Billings, too—if you decide that Hope isn't for you—I'd like to take you out to dinner."

"Dinner." She looked away.

"I told Chet how I felt about you," Andy said quietly. "You're my biggest regret. You're the one who got away. I know this is awkward and a little crass—"

He smiled hesitantly and she gulped in a breath.

"Andy, would you tell me what happened that night at the fair?" she asked.

Andy hooked a thumb through a belt loop. "I wish you'd just let that go."

"I can't. I need to know."

He nodded slowly, then shrugged. "I just hope you'll forgive me."

"Try me."

There was silence for a few beats, and then Andy took a deep breath and met her gaze. His eyes were sad, and she could tell this was difficult for him.

"Okay, well… I was cheating on you." He cleared his throat. "I was young and stupid, and I don't even know why I did it. I've regretted it for ten years. I never did it again. I didn't want to be that guy, but there it is. I'm sorry."

Somehow she wasn't surprised. She'd suspected it deep down, but having him confirm her suspicions still stung. So he'd been cheating on her while she'd been trying to find some sort of explanation that let him off the hook. Her mother had done the same thing for her father for years. It was an easy pattern to fall into, apparently.

Trust her gut—hadn't that been Chet's advice?

"Who was the girl?"

"She worked at the corner store. Her name was Tiffany. If it makes you feel any better, we only lasted a couple of months."

Tiffany from the corner store. Mackenzie shook her head. It was so ordinary. Was it that easy for men to betray the women who trusted them? Her father, now Andy... Granny had been right to keep this from her.

"I'm really sorry, Mack," he said. "You have to know that—"

"And Chet?" she interrupted. "You told me that he's the one who told you to break up with me. Is that really what happened?"

"He told me to choose," Andy admitted. "He said that I couldn't string you along, and that I needed to choose one of you. I knew he was right—I was already really guilty about it. I'm the moron who chose the wrong girl."

Did this change her feelings toward Andy? Not really, she realized. It helped to have an explanation, but it didn't leave her angry and betrayed the way she'd feared it might.

They stood in silence for a moment, and then he said, "I'm serious about that dinner, Mack. I know you've been getting closer to Chet lately, but I had to tell you how I felt. We could be good together, you and I."

"You aren't the same dumb kid that you were, Andy," she said softly. "And neither am I."

"So you forgive me?" he asked.

"I do."

And that was the truth. Forgiving him was easier than she'd imagined it would be. Enough time had passed. Enough had changed. This space between the tents was feeling stuffy now, and she was anxious to get out, get away. She wanted to get back to the ranch, go curl up on her grandmother's couch with one of her hand-stitched quilts and think. She had some choices to make, and she didn't exactly trust her mangled heart to make them.

"But I've got to go, Andy…" As she turned, she collided with someone tall and muscular. She looked up, startled. "Chet!"

Chapter 11

Chet rubbed the back of his neck with one work-roughened hand as he scanned the crowd. The truck had been fine—the lights turned off, as he remembered—and he knew this wasn't a coincidental mistake. It was the same old competition between him and Andy, and while they were both grown men, there was a spark of adolescence that never quite left a man, no matter how old he got.

Andy was making his move. It wasn't the idea of Andy asking her out that made his ire rise; it was the fact that he'd play some manipulative trick in order to do it. Andy wanted what he wanted, no matter who got hurt. He wanted to sell his land. He wanted another chance with Mack—

Okay, the thought of Andy and Mack together again did tick him off. But if being with Andy truly, deeply made her happy, he'd be able to get over it. Eventually. But he didn't think it would. Andy wasn't the guy for her, and Chet was tired of lurking in the background.

He spotted Mackenzie from behind. She stood in the space next to a ringtoss game and another tent. He knew her shape, the way her hair shone in the midway lights, the same way it had ten years before when he'd come sauntering through a fair in search of her—feeling more than he had any right to. Why couldn't that part have changed?

Her form was slim, and she glanced back, not far enough around to see him, and he found himself picking up his pace. He'd take her aside and talk to her—tell her all of it. It was high time, anyway.

Mackenzie took a step back just as Chet came up behind her, and she looked up at Chet in surprise as she collided with his chest.

"Chet!"

It was then that he saw his brother, and by the look on his face, they both knew what had happened here. He put his hands on Mack's shoulders and she moved aside easily enough.

"So you send me off to check on the truck to get some time alone with Mack?" he demanded.

Andy didn't answer, but a flush rising in his neck was confirmation enough.

"We aren't teenagers anymore, Andy!" he barked. "We're not the Granger boys. We're grown men."

"You were standing guard," Andy snapped back. "I did what I had to do to have a conversation without you there."

Doing what he had to do. That wasn't even a fair assessment. Chet had done what he had to do. He'd run the ranch, stayed behind when Andy went off to have fun and been the responsible brother when their father died. He'd taken care of everything, including Andy, only to have his brother waltz back into the picture and announce that he was tearing the ranch in half. Chet had had enough!

"Why did you even come back to the ranch?" Chet demanded.

"We're family," Andy snapped. "Remember that?"

"A lot that seems to mean to you." Chet raked a hand through his hair. "I've tried helping you—you won't take it. So what are you doing here?"

"Who asked you for help?" Andy challenged.

Chet blinked. "Isn't that what we do? You mess up, I clean up?"

"You don't see it, do you?" A look of disgust twisted his lips. "But then, you never did. All you care about is that bloody ranch."

"And why shouldn't I?" Chet barked. "It means something!"

"More than a brother does?"

Since when did it come down to a choice between his brother and his land? Andy was the one who'd walked away after their massive fight. Andy was the one who'd blocked his phone number so that he couldn't reach him. Andy was the one who'd decided that his part of the ranch wasn't enough. Chet hadn't made this about the land; Andy had.

"What, so if I cared about you, I'd sell the ranch my father left me?" Chet demanded.

"Left to you. That's what it amounts to. That entire cursed ranch was supposed to be yours. The fact that I got some pasture was just a formality." Andy spat on the ground. "You and Dad were exactly the same. You always cared more about the mud under your boots than you did about people. Mom wasn't happy with him. Did you even notice that?"

"She was happy." Chet grit his teeth. What would Andy have known about happy marriages? He was thirteen when their mother died, but his words brought up a wriggle of worry.

"How would you even know?" Andy said. "You were too busy with Dad to ever notice anything she felt. She was miserable. And that complete inability to see when a woman is unhappy is why you've been alone all these years, you self-righteous prig!"

Something inside Chet snapped at those words. It wasn't only the mention of his mother; it was the jab at his single status, too. Chet wasn't alone because he didn't have options—he was alone because the one girl who made his heart race had been off-limits. She still was. He loved this land, and his brother would tear it away from him out of sheer spite. Why he hadn't just done it already, Chet had no idea, but he was tired of waiting, tired of begging, tired of hoping that Andy would change his mind. If Andy was going to do it, he might as well get on with it, and Chet wasn't going to rein himself in any longer.

He didn't even feel it as he raised his fist,

and it was like watching it happen in slow motion as his knuckles connected with his brother's face. Andy staggered backward and came back with a right hook that left Chet's head ringing.

The fight was on. Chet hadn't gone against his brother since their teenage years, and it felt strange to be fighting him at this point of their lives. Andy hadn't spent the past decade doing manual labor, and it showed in his slower responses, but his younger brother still managed to get some solid hits in. Chet took three consecutive blows to the face before he let out a grunt of rage and slammed his brother back, launching Andy onto the ground, and he followed him down, landing on top of him, where he could slap away Andy's punches the way he had when they were kids.

"Stop it!" Mackenzie shouted. "Get off—"

Her words were swallowed up as Chet flipped his brother over and slammed his face into the ground. He'd used this move when he was a fourteen-year-old and his brother was twelve—it felt oddly satisfying to use it again. He held him still with a knee in his back.

"You think Mom was miserable?" he panted. "She wasn't miserable—she was sick! I knew about her cancer a full six months before anyone told you. That wasn't an unhappy marriage—that was grief, you little twit!"

"What is wrong with you?" Mackenzie's voice pierced his furious focus. He looked up to find her standing over there, her lips quivering with unspoken words. Her blue eyes snapped like crackling ice, and he found himself noticing wryly that he'd never seen her quite this beautiful.

"Get off me!" Andy growled from his position on the ground, but Chet didn't move.

"Sorry, Mack." Chet cast her an apologetic look. He hadn't meant to do this in front of her—he hadn't actually meant to do it at all, and as his blood began to slow, he knew that having her see him like this made it worse. This wasn't him—this wasn't the man he was day in and day out. This certainly wasn't the side of him he wanted her to remember when she thought of him.

"Let him up, Chet!"

"Not until I'm sure he's done," Chet replied, dabbing at his lip with the back of his sleeve. It came away bloody.

"I'm done, I'm done," Andy said, squirming against Chet's grip.

Chet released him, and Andy sat up, then rotated his shoulder, wincing. They both slowly rose to their feet. With the adrenaline seeping away, shame was taking its place. Chet wasn't proud of having just thumped his brother. They were grown men, and this was no way to resolve their differences. He knew that.

"So you all knew Mom was sick?" Andy said, his voice thick with emotion.

"Dad didn't want you to know," Chet said. "You were close with Mom. He didn't think you could handle it."

Andy shook his head and he eyed Chet with disdain.

"You and Dad and the land," Andy said, then spat some blood onto the ground. "Well, Dad's gone and now it's just you alone on some dirt. Not the same, is it? I said it before, and I'll say it again. You're alone for a reason. You put this stupid ranch ahead of everything that matters. You say family first, but you don't mean that. The land is first, and family comes second." He paused, then shook his head. "So stop trying to solve my problems and take a long look at your own."

His brother's words sank in slowly, and he hated the truth behind them. How long was he going to be cautious and responsible, ranching the land that would never keep him warm at night? Land and legacy mattered, but what happened when there was no one left to share it with or pass it down to? When did holding on to this ranch stop being worth the cost?

"Let's go home," Chet muttered. He tossed a handkerchief toward his brother, who let it drop on the ground. Andy used the back of his hand to wipe his bleeding nose instead.

"I'm not going anywhere with you." Andy shoved past him. "I was an idiot to come in the first place."

Andy stepped out into the flow of people and the jangle of gaming music.

"Andy!" Chet called, but his brother flatly ignored him and rounded the corner, heading back toward the concession, leaving Chet with Mackenzie, who didn't look entirely pleased with him, either.

"I'm sorry, Mack," he said. "I shouldn't have hit him. That was stupid."

"You better believe it was stupid!" Mackenzie looked as though her adrenaline was just starting to flow. "Look at you!"

"How bad is it?" he asked ruefully.

"Terrible. You're a bloody mess. What makes men think that pounding on each other is going to solve anything?" She picked up the handkerchief from the ground and turned to face him. He reached to take the handkerchief back.

"Stand still," she commanded. Chet obliged, and she reached up and dabbed at his eyebrow, wincing in sympathy every time she touched him.

"I'm fine," he said.

"You're an idiot, and you're not fine!" she shot back.

Chet caught her wrist in his grip and looked her in the eye. "I'm fine, Mack," he repeated. "I'm a big boy now."

Her expression softened, and as it did, tears misted in her eyes. She wasn't used to seeing that, he realized, and he felt bad that he'd exposed her to it. He released her wrist, and she looked down. He couldn't catch her eye again, and he wished that he could fix this with her somehow, show her that he wasn't the violent lout he appeared to be at the moment.

"We should get you back," she said, pulling her hair away from her face.

His jaw hurt and one of his teeth was loose—Chet had to admit to that—and he nodded in grudging agreement. He couldn't go around the fair looking like this, and he was pretty sure he was still bleeding from his lip.

"All right," he said on a sigh. "I'll get you home."

"What about Andy?" she asked.

"He's got friends here. He'll be fine," Chet said with a shake of his head. "He's not exactly a lost kitten."

"And for the record," Mack said testily, "I'm getting *you* home."

Chet smiled, and they headed back out toward the concession area and the front gates. One mother pulled a small child away from him as they passed, and guilt wormed its way up his belly. He certainly didn't want to freak out any kids, either.

As his boots hit the ground, he knew that everything was different now. It was over—whatever careful balance he and Andy had been holding was officially over. Andy was going to do whatever he had been planning to do all along, and Chet would have to live with the fallout.

Had he just lost his ranch?

"Mack," he said softly, and she looked up at him. "Thanks."

Just her being here while his life was about to implode—he was grateful for it. It was going to hurt, he had no doubt about that, but having her by his side, even if only for now, was more comforting than she'd ever guess.

Back in Granny's kitchen—her kitchen now—Mackenzie grabbed a cloth from a drawer by the big sink and turned on the tap. Outside the window, the night was dark and she could make out her own reflection in the glass—her hair tangled and her face as pale as the moon outside. She idly wished she looked better, but in comparison to Chet, she was a raving beauty at the moment, so perhaps it didn't matter much. She pointed to a chair by the table.

"Sit," she commanded, and Chet gave her a pained smile.

"Yes, ma'am."

She thrust the cloth under the cold water, then turned off the tap and squeezed it out. Not so long ago, she was the one being ordered around the kitchen for her blisters, and it felt good to be the one giving the commands for a change. She pulled another chair up to the cabinet so she could reach the first-aid kit, and when she got back down, she found Chet waiting for her, seated complacently with his big hands folded loosely in his lap. She put the first-aid kit onto the table beside her, and she took his face in her hands, examining the worst of the bruising.

"You're not going to be pretty tomorrow," she said.

"I wasn't pretty before," he said with a low laugh. "Go on. Do your worst on me."

Mackenzie began to gently dab and wipe away the dust and dried blood. He looked sadder than she'd ever seen him, and despite his size, he seemed somewhat deflated. This wasn't the Chet she knew.

"You could have hurt him worse than you did," she said.

"Yep."

"It's good you didn't."

Andy hadn't been a fair match for Chet, and at least Chet hadn't taken full advantage of that. He didn't say anything else, but that sadness remained. Those gray eyes were charcoal, and he flinched, pulling away as her cloth touched the bruising by his mouth.

"You two will make up," she said after a moment of silent work.

"Yeah?" Chet looked up at her, then back down. "I'm not so sure about that."

"Brothers fight," she said.

Chet didn't answer, and she knew it went deeper than that. From what they'd said to each other, she could see that their issues were much more deeply rooted than she'd ever realized, but when it came down to the line, Andy was there pleading his brother's cause. He wanted his brother to have his dream fulfilled, too. That was a loyalty not to be discounted.

"What did he want to talk to you about?" Chet asked after a moment.

Mackenzie sighed. "He asked me to sell my land to you."

The words hurt as they came out, because they had been confirmation of her suspicions all along.

"He what?" Chet caught her hand as she moved to wipe his face once more, and those darkened eyes met hers. "What did he say, exactly?" His voice was soft, but she could sense the urgency behind the words.

"He said he didn't want to leave you in the lurch and he was running out of time to sign if he was going to sell. So he wanted to know if I'd sell my land to you so that you could keep the ranch."

"That didn't come from me," he growled. "I didn't ask to buy you out."

"But it makes sense." She couldn't help the tremble in her voice.

Chet released her hand. He let out a long

breath as if he'd been holding it. Mackenzie put down the cloth and reached for some ointment in the first-aid kit. As she came toward him again, he put his warm hands on her waist and tugged her forward between his knees. His gaze was locked on her, and with one hand he took the ointment out of her fingers and deposited it onto the tabletop next to them.

"Chet—" she began, but she ran out of breath and out of words. She stood just taller than he was when he was seated, and he reached up and put his rough hand under her chin, tugging her face gently down toward his. He was a large man, and while the last time he'd kissed her he'd taken control, this time he waited for her to come to him.

"Chet, I—" she started again.

"Come here."

There was a gruff command in his voice, and this time she didn't want to defy it. When her lips touched his, he pulled her into the kiss and then down onto his lap. He slipped his arms around her slender waist, his mouth on hers. Her heart pounded, and she slid her hands up his hard muscular arms, stopping at his chest, where she pushed against him, pushing him back. His gray eyes had turned flinty black, and he looked ready to pull her back in if she didn't stand her ground.

"You've got to stop doing this to me," she whispered.

"Why?" he asked.

"Because I'm tired of having my heart put through the wringer with you Grangers," she said, and as the words came out, she felt tears rising up. Chet noticed the change in her, and he stared, leaning back.

"I'm not going to put you through the wringer," he said. He let go of her waist. "What did you think, that I'm here for your land? You should know me better than that by now. I don't want your land. What's more, I wouldn't buy it if you begged me."

She stood up, not wanting to stay quite so close—not like this. It was harder to form words when she could feel the very beat of his heart reverberating through his chest.

"He told me about the other girl," she said after a moment.

"Really?" Chet's eyebrows shot up. "I'm glad he did. Did he also tell you that I was telling him to choose between you, not to dump you?"

"He mentioned that," she said with a small smile.

"Helen was afraid that it would make it harder for you if you knew—considering your parents' situation at the time. She made me swear that I'd keep my mouth shut."

Mackenzie nodded. Such good intentions could be so incredibly frustrating.

"Mack—" he reached for her hand "—I would never do that to you. You know that, right? You can trust me."

Could she? It wasn't about Chet's fidelity or even about the land right now. This went deeper, to the thing that made Chet's heart beat—family. She might be able to trust Chet's good intentions, but he had no control over the impulses that drove him. He might not cheat, but there were other ways to lose a man.

"It can't work," she whispered.

"Why not?" He dropped her hand and she crossed her arms over her chest.

"If you and I started something between us—" Mackenzie swallowed, not even trusting herself with those words. She started again. "Chet, your brother told you how he felt about me."

"I love you more," he said simply.

Mackenzie blinked as she processed the words, and looking at the big cowboy with the sad eyes, she knew without a doubt that she loved him, too. But was love enough with-out family?

"He would never speak to you again," she said softly.

Sadness flitted across those rugged features, and he nodded slowly. "Possibly."

"And you could live with that?" she asked. "You'll have lost your father and your ranch, and you're willing to walk away from a rela-tionship with your brother, too?"

"What would you have me do?" Chet de-manded, anger sparking in his eyes. "Yeah, I'm losing a lot. Am I supposed to lose you, too?"

The thing was, Mackenzie didn't believe that Chet had to lose his brother. They were both angry, but Andy wasn't a complete jerk. He loved Chet, too, and right now they weren't just fighting over land; they were fighting over family history, childhood grievances and her. Andy would see a relationship as the last be-trayal.

"I know you, Chet," she said, a lump in her throat. "And you can't live happily without your brother in your life."

"I've managed it the past year." Chet pushed to his feet and walked to her kitchen window, looking out into the night.

"You're lying to yourself," she retorted,

shaking her head. "And if you and I start something, then Andy will walk away for good. You'll never see him again. Your dad isn't here to referee. No one is forced back to the dinner table together anymore—we're all grownups. That kind of thing turns into resentment, and you'll end up resenting me, too, because I'll be the reason for it all. You'll always regret this. Always."

Chet turned from the window and moved toward her. He stopped inches from her body, and he slowly ran his rough hands down her arms.

"Do you feel what I'm feeling?" His voice was low and soft, tempting and, oh, so inviting. "I'm in love with you. I think about you constantly. I'm not willing to hold back for Andy, or for anyone. I love you…"

If she told him no, then maybe he'd give it up and go back to sort things out with his family, but she couldn't bring herself to tell the lie. Denying her feelings would hurt more than declaring them.

"Yes," she whispered. "I do."

"Then what's stopping us?"

There were too many things standing between them, and while in this moment they both wanted to fall into the comfort of each other's arms, what about a year from now? What about another decade from now?

"Chet, I watched my father tear my family apart," she said, her voice shaky with emotion. "He did it for love—not one that lasted, might I add. But I hated that woman for tearing apart my home. My mother never really recovered. She's still broken from it, and I still feel sad for what we lost. I swore that I'd never be the one to tear apart someone's family—"

"You're no homewrecker, Mack," Chet said incredulously.

"Maybe not in the traditional sense," she agreed, "but if I give in to my heart, then it will end something that you need in order to be happy. You're a Granger, Chet. I don't care what your brother said about the land—your family means the world to you, and if you and I start something and Andy walks away for good, you'll regret this. You'll resent me. I can't do that to you."

"This is Andy's choice," Chet said, his voice thick. "Not mine."

"Maybe so," she agreed. "But no matter how angry you both are right now, you haven't passed the point of no return. You're still the Granger boys. You can recover from this. Brothers have tussled before."

Mackenzie picked up the ointment and put a dab on her finger. She gently touched the scrapes around his cheekbone with the medication. He allowed her to finish the job, and when she'd screwed the cap back onto the tube, she said, "Chet, I'll sell you my land."

Chet stared at her in disbelief. "No." His voice turned rough.

"What do you mean, no?" she asked. "I'm serious. Andy will sell your pasture—in fact, I think that's probably a guarantee now that you've beaten him up—and you can buy Granny's ranch from me. You'll have more than enough space. You'll even be able to expand a little."

"I'm not buying your ranch," he growled. "You wanted to run this place, and you should do that. I'll figure something out."

"I can't!" She shook her head, tears finally pricking her eyes. "Aren't you listening to me, Chet? I can't work next to you every day. I can't watch you move on with someone else!"

"Then don't!" he retorted. "Follow your heart!"

"Hearts break up families!" She could feel her tears wetting her cheeks as she searched his face for some sign that he understood what she was trying to tell him. "I can't be the one who stole your last chance with your brother."

"So you're decided?"

"Yes." Her emotions choked off the word.

Chet bent and pressed his lips hard against her forehead. He stayed there for a moment, as if he couldn't bring himself to pull away, but then he strode to the door.

"If you don't want me, that's okay," he said, and his voice trembled, betraying the depth of his feeling. "But I'm not buying your land, Mack, and that's final."

Chet pulled open the door and stepped outside without another backward glance. As the door shut behind him, Mackenzie sank down into a kitchen chair. The tears started to flow in earnest now, and her shoulders shook under the sobs that overtook her.

She'd never wanted to say yes so desperately in all her life, but as much as this hurt now, it would hurt even more if she faced Chet's angry, pained gaze once he'd realized that he'd lost his family for her. That was something she could never live with.

Chapter 12

The next morning after chores, Chet sat in his uncle's kitchen. Bob and Lydia Granger lived about fifteen miles away. The kitchen was old-fashioned, with a Formica countertop having been scrubbed so often that it had bare patches in the center of each stretch of countertop. It was polished to a clean shine, though, and everything smelled ever so faintly of bleach. Morning sunlight came in through the window, and the open back door let in a fresh breeze. It would have been a perfect morning for a coffee and a chat if Chet hadn't felt as if he'd been gutted.

Chet's phone lay on the kitchen table in front of him. It was turned on, an email glowing on the screen.

Hey, Chet. I've sold my land to the developer. He wants to buy yours, too, if you're interested. It's a done deal. I'm heading home to Billings. Andy

Such a short email to convey such a heavy message, and Chet sat there next to a half-filled mug of coffee feeling empty of emotion. It wasn't only this email that had scraped him out, though; it was how he'd left things with Mackenzie last night. His brother's email had just confirmed what he'd already known was coming.

He knew his ranch like the back of his hand, from the walk down to the barn to the ride to the summer pasture. He knew the lines of fence, the one stretch that needed mending every fall like clockwork, when every other line of fence stood up to the weather without problem. The rise and dip of the land, which looked so flat from a distance but wasn't flat in the least when you were riding across it—always either cresting a hill or thundering down the other side. He knew every copse, every stream, every dip and gully. The thought of tractors tearing through it, leveling it out and making muddy roads into it—that was painful. At the very least, his great-grandparents graves were on his property and not the pasture that his brother had just sold out from under him.

His aunt Lydia, a rotund woman with curly, graying hair, tutted her tongue softly from where she stood across the kitchen, her arms crossed over her chest. Beside her, a large tub of freshly picked strawberries sat ready for stemming. She would have picked them that morning before the heat of the day. His uncle Bob sat in the chair next to him, looking down at Chet's phone with a grim expression on his face. His knobby hands lay on the tabletop, motionless.

"Sold to the developer?" the older man muttered incredulously. "I told your father to leave the whole thing to you! I told him plain as day, and he said no, he couldn't do that to the kid. He said that Andy was sensitive. But that was years ago, and he should have updated that will…"

"Can't you talk to him?" Lydia asked. "He's your brother, after all—"

"It's done, Lydia," Bob said gruffly. "Once

there's a signature, it's done. There's no talking Andy out of anything."

"That young fool…" his aunt breathed.

Chet had nothing to say to that. His uncle and aunt had gone over this information a few times already, trying to make some peace with the fact that the Granger monopoly of land was about to be split up by some developer.

"Are you going to sell, too?" Bob asked suddenly.

"No," Chet said. "I'll die on that land before I sell it."

"Same here," Bob replied. "I've got about thirty acres of scrub I could let you graze on. It's not enough, but it's something."

"Thanks," Chet said hollowly. Thirty acres was not enough, but the gesture was a kind one. He'd have to figure out something, but having that land intact and pristine as they'd always known it was officially a thing of the past. The future was going to look different, no matter what he did now.

"So if Andy's selling, there might be others," Bob said. "Sometimes people you think would never budge are the first to jump at a fistful of money."

"And what about the girl?" Lydia asked. "Helen's granddaughter. Is she going to sell?"

"I'm not sure," Chet said. "She offered to sell to me, though."

Bob straightened at that. "You could have started out with that little nugget, Chet," he said. "Buy it. The property is adjacent, and it's excellent land."

It was excellent land. Helen's property was ideal in every way, and he'd offered to buy from Helen several times in the past, except that Chet refused to buy it from Mackenzie. Mack wanted to work that land, and she could do it, too. He wasn't going to be the one to take that away from her. It would be taking advantage of her emotional state, and one day he'd have to face God and he'd prefer not to have that one on his conscience. Besides, he was still hoping that she'd decide to stay.

Chet shook his head. "Not a chance. I'm not buying her land."

"Why on earth not?" Lydia demanded. Her hands seemed to work independently of the rest of her, stems flicking steadily into a pile in the sink. "You've been offering to buy that land for years. It's prime ranching land, Chet. You can't do better."

Chet was exhausted from a night of lying awake, and he had no energy to try to hide his feelings.

"Because I'm in love with her."

Lydia's hands stopped moving, and Bob and Lydia exchanged a look, and then both trained their gazes on him.

"I don't see the problem there," Lydia said after a second. "Then marry her."

Chet laughed bitterly. "If only it were so easy. She won't be with me because she thinks it'll drive a wedge between Andy and me."

"I think that wedge is pretty much driven," Bob pointed out. "And what does Andy care?"

"Andy thinks he's in love with her, too," Chet said.

"What on earth?" Lydia cried. "Wasn't he set to marry Ida?" She turned back toward the strawberries again. "No one said love was easy."

Bob sat in silence for a few moments, his eyes directed at his wife but his vision seemingly turned inward. Finally, he faced Chet and fixed him with a direct stare.

"If I understand you right, you've come for advice," Bob said.

"Yeah, that's right," Chet said.

"You've had a big shock, kid," Bob said. "If your dad were here, I'm sure he'd tell you the same thing. So it's hard to see the way when you've had a blow like this. But here's what you're missing—you need to buy that land from Mackenzie."

Chet shook his head. "Forget it. She'll think I'm just using her, and that's the last thing I'm doing when it comes to Mack."

"The heart can't lead you on this one," Bob said slowly. "Most times it can, but not this time. You've got to be logical. You can't run your ranch without that pasture, and if you have to sell off your herd, you're as good as out of the ranching business. Your only chance is to buy the Vaughn girl's land."

Chet sat in silence. He knew that his uncle was right. Bob was telling him only what every other member of this family would tell him— and they'd all be right, too. But he couldn't bring himself to do it. The logical answer wasn't always the one a man could live with.

"Bob is right," Lydia said. "You're a giving man, Chet. You've done a lot for your brother, and it's time to start taking care of yourself."

"If I took care of myself, I'd find a way to marry Mack," he said. "But if I do that... She's right, you know. Andy would walk away, and Dad isn't here to mediate between us or beg us to come home for Thanksgiving at the same time."

"I don't think Andy would walk away forever," Bob said. "He's a sensitive kid, but he was set to marry Ida up until... When did they break up, exactly? Anyway, that's not the point. He'll forgive you when he finds himself another woman. Period."

Was it as simple as that? He wanted to believe it, but he wasn't so sure.

"And since when has Andy ever stayed single long?" Lydia chimed in. "Mark my words, he'll have some young lady by Christmas, and it'll all be in the past."

He'd come for advice, and he'd gotten it. In fact, it was the very advice he'd expected to receive, but it still didn't feel any different when he rolled it over in his mind. If the pasture was going, maybe he needed to look at more permanent change. He pushed the chair back and stood up.

"Thanks, Uncle Bob, Aunt Lydia. I appreciate it."

"No problem, kid," his uncle replied, squinting up at him. "So what have you decided?"

Chet shot his uncle a grim smile. "I've got to make a call, but would you come by for supper tonight?"

Bob nodded slowly. "Could do. What's the plan?"

"I need someone on my side," Chet said. "And I know I can always count on you two."

Bob and Lydia exchanged another look, and Chet picked up his phone and started to dial as he headed out the back door for his truck.

"See you tonight!" he called over his shoulder.

Chet Granger wasn't beat yet.

Mackenzie stood at the fence, watching her grandmother's cattle graze. She'd done her chores on her own that afternoon, and when Chet had offered to help, she'd turned him down. She couldn't work shoulder to shoulder with him and keep her feelings under control—especially not now that she'd finally admitted to them.

The cows chewed in grinding circles, their tails flicking from time to time in the morning warmth. She'd miss this—the pastoral sweetness as the sun sank lower in the late-afternoon sky. She'd miss the smell of grass and cows, the far-off lowing of cattle. She'd miss standing with her boot hooked on the bottom rail of the fence.

She'd called her father that morning and asked if he could give her the information for the stable that was for sale. She wanted to do her own research and then set up a time to go see the place alone. If this was going to be her financial investment, then she needed to be sure of it, but it already looked promising.

The thought of leaving Chet behind wounded her. What was it with these Granger men that they managed to tear out her heart so efficiently? At least she'd managed to find out the truth about what had happened with her breakup with Andy, and that helped. She could firmly close the door on that chapter of her life. Closing the door on Chet, however, wouldn't be so easy. She couldn't work beside him day after day, or even watch him move on with someone who could make him happy without having it tear her heart out all over again. She couldn't be the reason he lost his brother, either, because she knew exactly how much those men needed each other. A woman could never take the place of a man's brother, and she wasn't foolish enough to try. Chet needed love, but he also needed family, and she'd never ask him to choose between them. So what choice did she have exactly? Did she love him? More than anything—enough to put herself through this heartbreak and leave town for good.

"I'm sorry I couldn't keep this place, Granny," she whispered. "I tried."

But she was grateful she'd been able to do what Granny had always wanted her to do, and that was to take control of her own life and future. She was doing that—using the sale of this ranch to finance another business. There would be no sitting around and waiting for her life to happen to her.

She looked over at the Granger barn, and her heart squeezed at the memories. She blinked back the involuntary tears and looked purposefully away again. Then she turned her steps back toward the smallest pasture, where the goats were grazing. Regardless of her own heartbreak or any of her future plans, there was a little chocolate-fleeced goat who needed a bottle of milk.

A few minutes later, Mackenzie sat on her haunches, holding the bottle still while Chocolate Truffle slurped back the last drops. She scratched the kid behind her ears and laughed softly at the tiny bleat.

"You're a cutie," she said quietly. "Go play with your brother."

The other kid—almost twice as big as the little brown doeling—was standing on top of Butter Cream's back where she lay on the grass, patiently chewing her cud while her baby used her as a jungle gym.

Mackenzie pushed herself to her feet, and as she rose, she saw Chet striding across the grass toward the pasture. Sadness welled up in her heart, and she went to the fence to meet him. She would miss seeing Chet like this most of all.

"Hi," he said, his smile warm and slow. "What are you up to?"

"Giving Chocolate Truffle her bottle," she said, waggling the empty bottle between two fingers. "How about you?"

"Come for supper." It sounded more like a command than a request, and she raised an eyebrow at him. "Please," he amended, his tone softening. "I'd really like it if you came for supper."

Mackenzie didn't have anything waiting in the house, and she paused for a moment. Maybe it was better to do things this way— have a proper goodbye. Loving Chet wasn't going to just go away, but perhaps she could still find a little closure.

Mackenzie bent and squeezed between the rungs of the fence, and then they walked together toward Chet's house. He scooped up her hand in his. She didn't pull away. They both knew where things stood, and his touch was firm and warm. She leaned into his strong arm, allowing herself this brief comfort.

"Will you change your mind and buy my land?" Mackenzie asked.

"Nope," he said, and there was no room for argument in his voice.

"Chet, I don't want to sell to the developer, but I have to sell." She slowed to a stop, forcing him to face her. "You won't keep me here by not buying it."

"Mack," he said seriously, "I'm not buying your land. You can sell it, or you can keep it, but I'm not buying it from you." He gestured toward the house. "I have some people I want you to meet."

"What?" She pulled back. If she'd known there would be other people here...

"Please, Mack." There was pleading in Chet's voice. "For me."

Mackenzie looked through the window and could make out a man and woman in their late sixties, by their appearance. They were sitting at the kitchen table, a deck of cards between them. She nodded, and they continued up the back steps and Chet pushed open the door.

The couple straightened and looked around as Chet and Mackenzie came into the house, and Mackenzie found herself immediately shy. There were more people here than just the older couple, people who hadn't been in view through the window. A younger couple with a baby sat on the other side of the table. A teenage boy stood in the doorway to the living room, and his attention was on his phone. She could hear some voices from the living room, too. The house was packed!

"This is my uncle Bob and aunt Lydia," Chet said. "That's my cousin Earl and his wife, Doreen. In there—" He laughed and shook his head, then raised his voice. "These are the Grangers. Everyone, this is Mack."

Chet had brought in some reinforcements, apparently, and she smiled nervously as they gave her polite nods and smiles. If only she knew what he was getting at. If he refused to buy her land, then what did he want? And why were all these people here?

"I wanted to ask you something," Chet said, pulling Mackenzie's attention back to him. His gray eyes fixed on hers. "I want to ask you this in front of everyone, because it involves them, too."

Mackenzie's gaze flickered to the older couple, who were now watching them with bated breath. The older woman nodded encouragingly, her hands clasped in front of her, and Chet touched Mack's cheek, drawing her gaze back to his.

"You don't want to be with me because you're afraid of driving my brother and me apart," Chet said. "But I wanted you to see everyone. This is my family, Mack. Some of them, at least. The ones closest to me."

Mackenzie swallowed hard. These were the Grangers, who always came first—who always would come first.

"You said before that we Grangers stick together, and you're right. We do. We're a family and belong together, but that doesn't mean that you don't belong, too. The thing is, family is messy. There's no getting around that, and they don't belong to me exclusively. This is also Andy's family, and they'll be there for him, too. This is a family that's big enough to share."

It was a kind gesture, but Mackenzie knew that there was a very big difference between being a family friend and being part of the family. He was a kind man who wanted to share the people in his life, but there were some things that couldn't be shared so easily.

"I'm not family," she said.

"But I want you to be," Chet said softly. "I want you to marry me. I want you to be my wife."

Mackenzie gaped up at Chet, staring at him in confusion.

"You want to…" Her words melted away.

"Mack, I've been in love with you for ten years," Chet said. "You know that. And being part of a family isn't always easy or clean, but it doesn't change who you are. My brother and I are at odds right now, but he'll always be my brother. Don't ask me to give up the one woman I've ever loved because of some family friction."

Mackenzie couldn't find the words, and she looked up at Chet, her throat thick with emotion.

"You love me, too, don't you?" Chet pressed.

Tears rose in Mack's eyes. "More than anything, Chet."

"Then marry me," he whispered.

She was silent for a moment, her thoughts on Andy, the brother Chet couldn't live without. What would happen to the Granger boys?

"And if Andy won't ever speak to you again?" she asked.

"He will." Chet's voice was firm, and then a small smile tickled his lips. "And if he doesn't, I'll return the favor and show up on *his* doorstep for a few weeks. We could do it together. We'll bring a sleeping bag to share and camp out in his living room until we grow on him. It would be kind of fun, don't you think?"

Mackenzie laughed softly. Chet's gray eyes sparkled down into hers, and then the smile slowly slid from his face, replaced with earnestness.

"Marry me, Mack."

She nodded, and her chin trembled. A whoop went up from the people who had now crowded into the kitchen, and Chet leaned closer, a smile shining in his eyes.

"I'm a stickler about these things. I wanted to hear the full request when you asked me to help you get started out here, and I want to hear the whole thing when you agree to marry me," he said with a slow grin.

"Yes, Chet," she said aloud. "I'll marry you."

Chet pulled her into his arms and his lips came down onto hers. The rest of the Grangers cheered and laughed, and there was the sound of some corks popping. Apparently, no one felt the need to wait for the happy couple.

When Chet finally pulled back, Mackenzie said, "And my land?"

"It's yours," he said softly. "Keep it or sell it. I'll run the stable with you if that's what you want. But whatever we do, I want to do it together—a joint venture—Chet and Mackenzie Granger against the world."

As Mackenzie stared up into Chet's gray eyes, she knew that in the arms of this stubborn cowboy, she'd finally come home. So she stood up on tiptoe and kissed him again, until someone thrust a glass of champagne into her hand and said, "Welcome to the family!"

And then she pulled back and looked around at the Granger clan's welcoming smiles.

"He'll be good to you," Uncle Bob said as she took the glass of bubbling champagne from his work-roughened fingers. He winked. "And if he gives you any grief, you tell me."

Mackenzie laughed and slipped her hand into Chet's strong grasp. Chet Granger just might be the last principled man under sixty. She had a feeling that his arms were the safest place she'd ever know.

Epilogue

The Elks' Hall was located outside town on a rural road. A verdant field spread out behind the old wooden building, and a stretch of trees rustled in the breeze beside it. After a winter that had felt endless to Chet as he and Mackenzie planned their wedding, this spring Sunday was warm, fragrant and perfect.

The wedding itself had taken place at the church in town, and they'd gone afterward for a picture-taking session with the photographer, and now they were at the hall, ready to celebrate with family and friends. Mackenzie was laughing with a group of young women who were fingering her long lace veil admiringly. A bridesmaid perched beside Mackenzie said something, and they both looked into the bridesmaid's phone to take a selfie together.

She made a stunning bride—her cheeks pink from laughter and her vintage lace dress clinging to her curves. She glanced over her shoulder in Chet's direction, and he thought his heart would burst from sheer love.

Chet and Andy stood a few yards off, dressed in their wedding tuxes, flowers in their buttonholes. The rest of the guests were milling about, getting ready to go inside and start the festivities, and the brothers had taken a few minutes to talk—something that they hadn't managed until now. Wedding photos and all that posing were surprisingly demanding.

"There's something that's been eating at me," Andy said after a few seconds of silence. "The pasture. I'm not sorry I sold it, but I wasn't going to do it that way. I was going to give you time to figure out something else first—size up some land, make some decisions—"

"It's okay." Chet had been angry. He couldn't pretend that he hadn't been, but it had all worked out. Mack had chosen to keep her land after all, and they were ranching together— shared land, shared herd, shared life.

"All the same, I'm sorry," Andy said. "I was mad and I acted rashly. I don't want to be that guy."

"You had dreams, too, and that land was your inheritance. I get it."

"Thanks." Andy was silent for a moment, and the brothers' eyes moved toward Mackenzie, who was leaning on a bridesmaid while another fixed something on her delicate white shoe. She balanced there for a moment, then put her foot down. She was exquisite—and she'd gone from cowgirl to heels. He'd never stop being amazed by her.

"You're a lucky man," Andy said with a nod.

"Thanks." Chet had to agree—he was infinitely more than lucky.

"I know you think I was nuts not to marry Ida." Andy ran a hand through his auburn hair.

"Yeah, I did." Chet cast his brother a wry smile.

"She just got married two weeks ago." Andy glanced toward the road, where some more cars were turning in. "Did you know that?"

"I'd heard." It hadn't seemed kind to mention it. "So who's the guy?"

"His name is Calvin," Andy said. "Owns a restaurant in Billings. They met when she went for dinner with some friends, she said.

They both just seemed to know—right away. She and I were never like that. There was always a lot of uncertainty and doubt."

"All the same, I'm sorry." It couldn't be easy for Andy to watch Ida move on, after all the time they'd been together.

"I'm happy for her," Andy replied. "I can't begrudge her happiness. We were broken up, after all. She's kind and sweet. She deserves this—even if I wasn't the guy to give it to her. Besides, it gives me the kick in the pants I need."

"Yeah?" Chet shot his brother a curious look. "How so?"

"I want what Ida found," he said. "I want what you and Mack have. I want the real thing."

Chet nodded slowly. "It's worth the wait, man."

"I believe it." Andy grinned at his brother and slapped him on the back. "Now I have to get ready for my best-man speech. Go find your beautiful bride."

Mackenzie turned away from the women again, and her sparkling blue eyes caught his. He'd leave his brother to his last-minute speech writing, and hopefully, Andy wouldn't come up with any memories that were too embarrassing. Chet headed across the grass toward Mackenzie and slipped his arm around her slim waist. She leaned into his embrace and tipped her head onto his shoulder. The delicate scent of her perfume wafted around him.

"Mrs. Mackenzie Granger," he murmured in her ear. "I'm never going to get tired of that."

"You'd better not," she said with a soft laugh. "Because you're stuck with me from now on."

"Come on," Chet said, tugging her toward the door. "I can't wait to get in there and dance with my wife."

Mackenzie slid her hand into his, and he could feel the sharp press of her rings against his callused hand. He'd remember this—these details, like the feel of her rings against his fingers, the smell of her perfume, the way her veil fell down her back, billowing out like the clouds that sailed over the rolling Montana plains. He'd remember this, and one day he'd tell his son what it felt like to have all his dreams come true on the day he married the girl the next ranch over.

* * * * *

Get 4 FREE REWARDS!

We'll send you 2 FREE Books plus 2 FREE Mystery Gifts.

FREE Value Over **$20**

Both the **Harlequin® Historical** and **Harlequin® Romance** series feature compelling novels filled with emotion and simmering romance.

YES! Please send me 2 FREE novels from the Harlequin Historical or Harlequin Romance series and my 2 FREE gifts (gifts are worth about $10 retail). After receiving them, if I don't wish to receive any more books, I can return the shipping statement marked "cancel." If I don't cancel, I will receive 6 brand-new Harlequin Historical books every month and be billed just $5.69 each in the U.S. or $6.24 each in Canada, a savings of at least 12% off the cover price or 4 brand-new Harlequin Romance Larger-Print every month and be billed just $5.59 each in the U.S. or $5.74 each in Canada, a savings of at least 14% off the cover price. It's quite a bargain! Shipping and handling is just 50¢ per book in the U.S. and $1.25 per book in Canada.* I understand that accepting the 2 free books and gifts places me under no obligation to buy anything. I can always return a shipment and cancel at any time. The free books and gifts are mine to keep no matter what I decide.

Choose one: ☐ **Harlequin Historical**
(246/349 HDN GNPD)

☐ **Harlequin Romance Larger-Print**
(119/319 HDN GNQD)

Name (please print)

Address   Apt. #

City   State/Province   Zip/Postal Code

Email: Please check this box ☐ if you would like to receive newsletters and promotional emails from Harlequin Enterprises ULC and its affiliates. You can unsubscribe anytime.

> **Mail to the Harlequin Reader Service:**
> **IN U.S.A.:** P.O. Box 1341, Buffalo, NY 14240-8531
> **IN CANADA:** P.O. Box 603, Fort Erie, Ontario L2A 5X3

Want to try 2 free books from another series? Call 1-800-873-8635 or visit www.ReaderService.com.

---

*Terms and prices subject to change without notice. Prices do not include sales taxes, which will be charged (if applicable) based on your state or country of residence. Canadian residents will be charged applicable taxes. Offer not valid in Quebec. This offer is limited to one order per household. Books received may not be as shown. Not valid for current subscribers to the Harlequin Historical or Harlequin Romance series. All orders subject to approval. Credit or debit balances in a customer's account(s) may be offset by any other outstanding balance owed by or to the customer. Please allow 4 to 6 weeks for delivery. Offer available while quantities last.

Your Privacy—Your information is being collected by Harlequin Enterprises ULC, operating as Harlequin Reader Service. For a complete summary of the information we collect, how we use this information and to whom it is disclosed, please visit our privacy notice located at corporate.harlequin.com/privacy-notice. From time to time we may also exchange your personal information with reputable third parties. If you wish to opt out of this sharing of your personal information, please visit readerservice.com/consumerschoice or call 1-800-873-8635. **Notice to California Residents**—Under California law, you have specific rights to control and access your data. For more information on these rights and how to exercise them, visit corporate.harlequin.com/california-privacy.

HHHRLP22

Visit
ReaderService.com
Today!

As a valued member of the Harlequin Reader Service, you'll find these benefits and more at ReaderService.com:

- Try 2 free books from any series
- Access risk-free special offers
- View your account history & manage payments
- Browse the latest Bonus Bucks catalog

Don't miss out!

If you want to stay up-to-date on the latest at the Harlequin Reader Service and enjoy more content, make sure you've signed up for our monthly News & Notes email newsletter. Sign up online at ReaderService.com or by calling Customer Service at 1-800-873-8635.

RS20